MW01492244

Published

by

VYSS Publishing

Copyright © 2013 by

Makenzi

ISBN-13: **978-0-9898910-1-1**

Library of Congress Control Number: 2013915689

Printed in the United States of America

10 9 8 7 6 5 4 3 2 1

Dedication

This book is dedicated to everyone who has supported me. I truly appreciate the love and support, it does not go unnoticed.

Much love,

Makenzi

Wicked

Attraction

PROLOGUE

Up until now, I had been able to keep all information about Mark, my youngest uncle, to myself. As far as I knew, Mark, my grandmother, and I were the sole keepers of the secrets. And secrets we had. I would have gone to my grave with them as my grandmother did, but since I told Dr. Wardelle that I wanted to reach out to Carmen, he suggested that I use a letter to open the doors of communication. It took me about a month to finally get my thoughts together on what I wanted to write, and I came to the realization that I wouldn't be able to protect the secret any longer. A part of me didn't want to dredge up this entire situation, but Carmen needed to know how fucked up my life had been and that yes, I blamed her for everything. There was no way to really tell her about me without telling her about Mark. She had to know that I clung to him, along with others, because I was afraid of being abandoned once again. She had to know that I led a life of complete destruction because I'd never really felt loved.

Dear Carmen,

I'm sure you're surprised to be receiving a letter from your daughter after all these years. You do remember that you have a daughter whose name is Christian Alicia Johnson, from Detroit; father's name is Melvin Johnson? It took a lot of my time and money to find you. I hope that in the near future we can talk face to face, but I think a letter will do for now. I had a private investigator find you, and since the day he told me he located you, I have spent many

2

long sleepless hours crying, wondering if I should actually contact you.

Carmen, or Mom, not sure what the fuck to call you at this moment, you birthed me, so by the law of the land, you are considered my mother, but because I don't know you, I'm not even sure why I give a fuck about you. You are a selfish ass individual; the only thing you did was carry and birth me. My daddy did everything else; he raised me and a fine job he did. You walked your funky ass right out of my life and never looked back. If I hadn't looked for you, I would have died never knowing my mother. Have you even taken two seconds to think about me? That's fucked up; I was your first born.

I have a lot of things running through my mind right now. I just have so many questions. I'm not going to sugar coat anything as there is no easy way for me to express my feelings as I am sure you can tell. So I will only be me and

3

that is straightforward; there has already been so much time wasted. The first question I would like to ask you is why you left me when I was just a child. That wasn't fair. I didn't ask to be born into this world, and I damn sure didn't ask to be left alone without a mother in my life. What child doesn't even know what their mother looks like? Can you imagine how hard growing up without you was for me? The only pictures I have of you are so old, and I know you have changed many times since then. When my friends would ask me what you looked like, I just lied and made up my own version. I imagined you'd be a prettier version of me. But after years of counseling, I realize that's just what I wanted you to be.

People always asked me where you were. They wanted to know why you didn't live with us. Little did they know I didn't know where the hell you lived let alone why you didn't live here with us. The only place I knew about

4

was D.C., and my aunt Whitney told me you died in the streets in California. Although I didn't know you and you had certainly thrown me away like yesterday's news, I didn't appreciate her gossiping about you. Imagine that, here I am going off on my aunt who, although has her ways, was way more of a mother to me than you ever were. You see how fucked up you got me, Carmen? I haven't been right since you left, and yes, bitch, I am blaming it all on you! You might wonder why my words are so strong, and as I am writing and re-writing this letter, I want to soften my verbiage, but I can't. I am so damn angry right now. You have no idea what I've been through over the years, no idea. I want to hurt you the same way you hurt me. I hope you are crying your eyes out right now. I hate you...I hate you...I hate you... Why didn't you just abort me? I was born into a fucked up situation, I swear!

Did your ignoring my existence bother you? It still bothers the hell out of me. Did you ever cry, feel sad, and wonder if I was okay? Damn, did you feel any kind of way about leaving my father alone to raise me? Please tell me you did. Please tell me that you agonized over leaving me. Please explain that there is some extenuating circumstance that kept you from coming back for me. Tell me that you tried, but someone or something wouldn't let you. Just please don't tell me that you didn't care. I don't think I can handle that, Carmen. Don't tell me that you just didn't give a damn about your firstborn child. You didn't have to love my daddy. Whatever reason you didn't want to be around him was between you and Mel. But me, on the other hand, I was a different story. Well at least I should have been. You didn't know if another woman would accept me as her own. You didn't know if my father would mistreat me growing up.

You didn't know anything, and from your actions, you didn't give a damn.

Well, my father did not mistreat me growing up. As a matter of fact, he raised me very well. He provided me with everything from the best schools to expensive clothes. We went on elaborate vacations each summer. Christmas at our house looked like a major department store. At 16, he bought me a brand new Toyota Celica because that's what I had to have. I had fur coats, diamonds, designer purses, and sunglasses – simply everything. I think he gave me everything that I assume he would have given to you. People always questioned the way he raised me. They thought we were "too close." They don't know that I heard them when they would whisper that they thought we had an inappropriate relationship because he was so doting. They didn't think a man should treat his daughter the way he treated me.

They were worried about the wrong man.

What I am about to tell you is very difficult for me. I don't tell people this shit. I haven't even told my daddy. As close as Daddy and I are, I kept it from him because I knew he'd kill anyone who hurt me. Literally. See my daddy loved me just that much. You can't even imagine that type of love, can you? I'd already lost you; there was no way that I was going to let my father go to jail. Unh, unh, I wasn't going to be responsible for that. Yep, you're wondering what the hell I am talking about, aren't you? Don't worry about it, Carmen. I took it like a big girl. I had to, that's all I know how to do is take the hand that I is dealt and play the hell out of it.

Do remember my uncle Mark? One of Mel's brothers, he was the baby of the family. Really handsome, like Mel, looks exactly like my daddy. He's my favorite uncle, with his cool ass. He took me everywhere with him. He was more like my big brother than my uncle. Funny thing is he remembered a lot about you, definitely more than I did. He is the only one besides Aunt Whit who really talked to me about you.

Mark and I were so close. He babied me. He'd let me sit on his lap. Heck, I didn't see anything wrong with it; I mean I still sat on Mel's lap. But I soon learned that sitting on my daddy's lap was not the same as sitting on Mark's.

I started to feel something different when on Uncle Mark's lap. I now know what I was feeling was an erection. That made me curious. Don't judge me, shit, I was young. I asked him what it was, and he asked me if I wanted to see it. He was young, too. Yep, I sure did want to see it. You would have thought I would have run or been grossed out, but I wasn't. I thought, wow, that was different from what I had between my legs. Though inappropriate, it didn't bother me in the least. I was so naïve, I didn't know any better, but I am sure Mark did. To make a long story short, around the family, we were normal uncle and niece, but every chance we got to be alone, he used my body for his pleasure, and I didn't mind. I was in love with my own uncle.

You know what? Grandma knew this was going on. When I had to stay over there with them on the weekends, even though I could sleep in the guest room, she didn't object when Uncle Mark said I should sleep in his room. He had twin beds, but she knew we slept in the same bed because she walked past the room one time and saw that nigga on top of me and didn't say a thing. She actually turned her head. If I didn't know any better, I think she looked at me in disgust, like it was somehow my fault that her precious son had been "loving me" for years.

Nobody but my daddy care about me, damn.

Well, I think Mark cared, too. Yeah...he cared. But Grandma, she even took me to the abortion clinic when my stomach began to grow because she certainly didn't want my father to find out about me and his baby brother. He'd always accused her of favoring Mark anyway, and she knew he would kill her, too, if he knew. On the ride to the clinic, she talked some shit to me about not letting any boy have his way with me. She told me that I had to be more careful. Any boy? Was this bitch serious?

"Grandma, it was your damn son" is what I wanted to say. But there was no need to say shit, she knew. Instead of Grandma talking to Mark and letting him know that what he was doing was wrong, she put me on birth control, sort of "okaying" me and Mark's fuckfest as long as it didn't result in another unplanned pregnancy. I know she told him that I was on birth control because before he would use a condom sometimes, but after I had the abortion, he never did. So trust that Grandma and I were on a first name basis with the receptionist at the abortion clinic. I spent the majority of my

11

teenage years pregnant, and as soon as I hit the eight-week mark, she'd schedule me an appointment and not less than three to four months later, Mark would knock me up again. It was kind of fun to watch the bitch scramble to come up with the money to pay for all those damn abortions. She was something else. It might make you feel a little better to know that I actually hate her ass more than I hate you. May that bitch rest in hell.

Funny thing is I thought me and Mark were in love. I didn't really realize how wrong that shit was until I was much older. Do you know that I was actually hurt when he got a girlfriend and stopped "loving" me? I was beyond depressed. I hated Mark, not for the inappropriate relationship, but for cutting it off. Isn't that some sick shit, Carmen? I welcomed and encouraged being molested by my father's baby brother?

Although my daddy didn't know what was wrong with me, his mammy did. Did she comfort me? Hell no, she told me I was a whore like you! She actually called me to tell me how happy she was that Mark had finally turned his attention to someone else. Isn't that all but admitting that she allowed this bullshit? She suggested that I find some other little nigga to fuck with and that's exactly what I did. Thanks for giving me permission to become an easy lay, Grandma. I owe you one.

I still see Uncle Mark at family functions. There's still something weird between us, but we've both learned how to act "normal," whatever the hell that means. I'm not a perfect person, but after all that I've been through, I'm not a bad person, and I damn sure didn't deserve the repercussions of your decision to abandon your responsibility, me. You should have been the one to help me transition into a woman, but I guess you couldn't help me

13

become a woman because you weren't one. A real woman wouldn't have walked out on her responsibilities. I couldn't imagine leaving my kids under any circumstances. Yep, I have kids. After a million trips to the abortion clinic, I vowed that I would become a mother and that I wasn't going to let anyone keep me from that ever again. I won't go into anything further about my kids because I am not sure if I want to let you into that very personal part of my life. But know this, not having a mother screwed me up in more ways than I can count, but the one thing it did not do was ruin my ability to be a good mother to my children. I guess the apple can fall far from the tree. There are so many other deplorable things that have happened to me over the years. I feel like I have paid the price for all of your sins. You owe me, Carmen, whatever your name is: You owe this bitch Christian big time.

CHAPTER 1

Dr. Wardelle had become like my best friend. He knew all the messed up stuff that I'd done, and he had never judged me. Not once. He was like that best girlfriend that everyone needed, the one who truly listened. He understood that even though I believed my father loved me, I was having a hard time separating his true feelings from his feelings of obligation to me: There's a difference.

"Feeling abandoned is the worst feeling in the world, and no matter how hard anyone tried to fill the void, their efforts were useless," I said barely above a whisper. "There is just no getting over being abandoned by your mother. My daddy did his best, but he was young and handsome and had tons of women over all the time. Because I didn't like any of them, I was forced to spend a substantial amount of time at my grandparents' house while the women spent a lot of time at our house with my dad. All of my aunts and uncles were out of the house either in college or married except for my uncle Mark. So he became my unofficial babysitter."

Dr. Wardelle had let me go on for a short while uninterrupted; I took a deep breath and turned toward the window. I just couldn't look him in the face right now. I drifted into deep thought as I went back down memory lane. I wanted to lie. After all that had happened between me and Mark, there was no way I should be able to still speak of him in a favorable light. But I guess it's true, you sure can't help who you love. I hated to think about this, let alone talk about it. I was so ashamed of my feelings. It was true, my uncle made me feel special even when we slept together. I loved him. I knew I should've hated him because I was a child, and I was his niece, but I didn't. I still loved my uncle to this day, which was why it was so hard for me to tell Dr. Wardelle all about our secrets.

Dr. Wardelle noticed my apprehension because he asked me if I wanted to take a break. I didn't. I only wanted to discuss this Mark thing one time. I knew if we took a break, I would have to come back and continue to tell him how much I still loved my uncle. How I couldn't hate him even though I wanted to; it would make my life easier. So, this time I shook my head, and he continued with his questions.

"I made it my goal to have sex with Mark every other day, no matter what I had to do. There were times when his girlfriends would be over, and I knew he would be having sex with them upstairs while he made me go downstairs and play Nintendo, but as soon as he'd walk them to the door,

I'd run upstairs and get in his bed. He was a guy. It wasn't like he was going to turn me away.

"There were times when I met him at the high school and had sex with him in the gym after his basketball practice. We had sex in my grandparents' car, one time we even had sex in my father's bed."

Tears fell. All I could think about was how sick and twisted I must be to have lusted after my own flesh and blood like that.

I turned and glanced at Dr. Wardelle. His face read one word: shock. He actually looked sympathetic. He'd known me long enough to know that I was sick, plain sick and needed help. Up until now, I didn't realize how much this thing with Mark messed with my mind.

I don't think he meant to sound disappointed, but I heard it in his voice, after I told him about making love to Mark in the backseat of my car in the parking lot of the reception hall at his own wedding. How he forced himself on me and... loved me. I remembered Mark being so rough, like he had something to prove. I prayed that it would be over soon, not that I didn't enjoy it, because I did, but I was deathly afraid that someone would find us. Mark was doing things to me that he had never done to me before. He kept saying that he wanted to get me pregnant again. Saying all types of stuff, then it was over. I actually felt like I had the upper hand, I had the power. I was powerful enough to make a newly married man leave his wife alone in their reception and come make love to me in a car right underneath the noses of over 500 guests!

Dr. Wardelle wrote quickly in his tablet. He was probably trying to keep up with all this mess I was feeding him. I loved Mark and I loved the idea that he couldn't stand to be away from me. I loved the fact that although he had a wife he still desired to be with me. When I left for college, he sent me money all the time. For Christmas and birthdays, Mark gave me a credit card and told me to use it for my leisure as long as I saw him when I came home for visits.

I was telling Dr. Wardelle things that I had never told anyone. What type of woman slept with her own uncle? What type of woman became pregnant with her uncle's babies? I took money and gifts from him in exchange for sex. I was basically a prostitute for him, and I didn't care.

By now, I was crying uncontrollably. Knowing what a mess I was one thing, but actually saying it aloud was altogether different. The more I thought about it, the madder I became at having included any of this in my letter to Carmen. I couldn't risk it coming out. Nah, I couldn't take that chance. I was panicking at the thought. Dr. Wardelle tried to comfort me a little by reassuring me that I didn't have to share anything that I didn't want to. He kept reminding me that I was in control of my life now, not Mark and not Carmen.

"Christian, I think we can wrap up for today," he said as I stood and walked toward the window. "But, I do have one last question for today." Ever so quietly, he asked, "Do you still see your uncle?" I knew he meant *see* as in had we slept together.

"It's been awhile," I said, ashamed of what I was admitting to the man who saved my marriage a few years back.

"What's awhile, if you don't mind me asking?"

I took a huge breath and told this counselor, someone that had become one of my most trusted confidantes that the last time I slept with my uncle was nine months to the day before my first child was born.

CHAPTER 2

Two months later

" "Flight 1210 heading to Los Angeles will now begin boarding," the female attendant announced. As I handed her my ticket and boarded the plane, I became completely nervous. I couldn't believe it. After all the trouble I went through, in a few hours, I could possibly be face to face with Carmen. Dr. Wardelle agreed with my decision to fly out to California; he thought it was a great idea as long as I could handle the fact that Carmen might reject my visit. As I sat in my seat and waited for the other passengers to board, a part of me felt like I should have listened to my father when he told me several times to leave that door shut, but me being me, I couldn't leave well enough alone.

My mind constantly raced back and forth with thoughts of rejection that Carmen might place upon me. I couldn't get those painful memories out of my mind ever since I opened the lines of communication with her. Was she happy to receive a letter from me? Did she even receive my letter? Was she going to contact me? Why didn't she respond to my letter? Was she in fact dead and the private investigator I hired wrong?

Every day for the last two months, I secretly hoped for a response from Carmen, but I never received one. I included my phone number, the house and beauty salon numbers, Kory's cell number, and even my email address and still no response.

Six hours later, when my plane landed in the LAX airport, I grabbed my Michael Kors purse and walked off the plane.

I pulled out my cell phone and called Kory, and after three rings, he finally answered.

"Hey, baby, my plane just landed. I will call you when I check into the hotel, love you."

"Okay, baby. I'm glad you made it. Have a good time and be safe. If some shit jumps off, call me, and I'm on the next thing smoking headed to California. Love you, too." I laughed as we ended our call because I knew Kory wasn't playing. He was very protective of me and the kids.

After I picked up my luggage from baggage claim, I walked outside and flagged down a taxi.

"Take me to the Marriott on Beverly Hills Drive." If everything worked out as planned, Enterprise was supposed to have a rental car waiting for me at the hotel.

So far everything was working in my favor; my plane ride was good, my room was ready when I arrived at the hotel, and Enterprise had my Toyota Camry waiting for me in the hotel parking lot. After I dropped off my bags and freshened up a bit, I went downstairs to the business center to MapQuest Carmen's address. I printed the directions, walked out the hotel doors, jumped in the rental car, and drove the twenty minutes it took to drive to Carmen's house.

I called Kory as I was pulling up to Carmen's apartment. "Okay, babe, I'm outside her apartment. This shit looks raggedy as hell." I laughed.

"Please be careful, Chris," Kory begged, turning the call back to serious.

"I will, I promise. If some shit goes down, I will be out of there." I closed my cell phone as I approached the apartment, feeling as if I was about to have a panic attack. My heart was beating more than normal, and my palms were starting to sweat. This neighborhood looked just like a scene from *Boyz n the Hood* or *Menace II Society*; this was definitely the projects, a place I wouldn't be living.

I've replayed the scenario a million times or so in my head since I was a little girl, around the age of seven or eight years old. I'd run up to Carmen, tell her how much I missed not having her in my life, we'd hug, cry and live happily ever after. But for thirty plus years, it hadn't played out that way, but hopefully things would change today.

Taking a deep breath, I leaned in and slowly knocked on the door. Moments later, I heard a female voice speak "Who is it?" As the door swung open, my heart began beating faster. "Can I help you?" A female wearing a floral print pink and yellow dress holding a cane stood holding the door partly opened.

"Does Carmen Johnson live here?" I tried to keep a smile on my face at least until I was sure it was Carmen that was standing in front of me.

"Yes, that's me," she replied, looking distastefully at my face as if she was trying to figure out who I was and why I was at her door.

"I'm Christian, your daughter." The door opened widely, and Carmen stepped aside, letting me in. I stood in the doorway and closed the door slowly behind me as I took a look at the mess inside of the apartment in front of me. Carmen reached out her arms, motioning for me to hug her. We stood there in the doorway, hugging, for what seemed like forever. I broke from our embrace, staring Carmen in her face; she was a pretty lady, but the bags under her sunken eyes made her look tired and kind of old. She looked as if she might be sick and nothing like I had pictured all these years. Her body was slender and fragile, making her look as if she was about five feet in height.

I had no clue what to say. I stood there and looked at Carmen, and she did the same. "Christian, have a seat. Move those clothes on the floor and sit right there on the couch." Carmen spoke as she struggled to sit down in the brown recliner chair that should have been in yesterday's trash.

I felt my heartbeat thumping. "How are you?" I asked, feeling sick to my stomach, but I continued to remind myself that I was there for a purpose, and I needed to calm down.

"I'm living, so I guess all right. I received your letter. I couldn't write back because MS has taken over my body, makes my whole body ache constantly."

I stared at Carmen with my nose scrunched up, "MS, what's that?"

"Multiple Sclerosis."

"How long have you had that?"

"It started really messing with me after I gave birth to Meko, but over the years, it has gotten worse. Some days I can't even get out the bed."

I suddenly felt lightheaded. I was tired of pretending all the time that I was alright, when I really was just unhappy, and more confused than I had ever been in my life. I plastered the familiar fake smile I had been using lately on my face and began to speak. "So you have another child?"

"Yes, Kameko, and she gets on my damn nerves. She at that age... twenty-one, all she does is party all the time. She should be running her fast ass in here sometime soon."

Anger centered itself in my chest. Carmen was talking to me like there wasn't an elephant in the room. *How in the hell can you walk out on one daughter, but turn around and have another child?*

Carmen struggled to get out of the recliner; she walked in the kitchen. "Christian, would you like a beer?" she yelled into the living room.

"No thank you," I replied as she made her way back into the living room with a can of Miller High Life. Carmen sat back down, barely taking her lips off the beer can she was holding.

The silence in the room was very uncomfortable until Carmen decided to speak.   "How's Melvin?"

"He's good." I tried to keep my answers as short as possible when it came to my father. He damn near threatened to cut me off when I told him I was coming to California to meet Carmen.

"Do you have any other sisters or brothers?"

"Nope, I'm the only one, Daddy's little lady." I had to think of something and quick to take the subject off my father. I replayed his words in my mind: "Christian, don't discuss shit about me to that woman, you hear me?"

"Does your father still live in D.C.?" I asked.

Carmen shook her head no as she started coughing really hard, sounding like she had smoker's cough. "My father passed away about ten years ago."

"I'm sorry to hear that. What happened?"

"He was in a car accident, had a heart attack, hit a pole, and died right there on the scene. I refused to go to the funeral because I felt uncomfortable being around my own family. I never like none of them. They all phony."

I stared at Carmen because I wasn't sure where this conversation was going plus that damn cough of hers was driving me crazy. Why would she miss her own father's funeral? I don't care where I was in the world; I would never ever miss my daddy's funeral unless I left this earth before he did.

"I hated that man," she said. "He controlled everything I did, who I talked to, where I went, how I moved, that's why I was so happy when I got married and was able to move away. I wanted my freedom. There were no witnesses when he had the accident, so I assumed his death came quickly, and I want to believe he didn't feel any pain."

When Carmen spoke, I almost wanted to reach out and give her a hug because she spoke like she did truly hate her father, probably the same way I hated her.

"Wow that's deep." I didn't want to say too much because right now Carmen was talking non-stop, her mouth moving like Dunn's River Falls in Jamaica. My purpose was to find out as much as I could about her in the time frame that I would be here in California.

"I pretended to cry over the phone when my aunt called me. I didn't give a damn that he was dead. I hadn't talk to him in about twenty years before then. Christian, those people don't care about me. My own family put me in shit that I didn't have anything to do with."

Our conversation was interrupted when the front door swung open, and three females piled into the room.

"Meko, this is your sister Christian. Christian, that's Meko," Carmen blurted out, then took a gulp from her can of beer.

"Hello," I replied, giving Meko the once over; she looked nothing like me. Her almond-shaped eyes and thick eyebrows clearly made her look more Asian than black. Her hair was jet black and silky straight draped down to her butt. She was cute, and her facial features clearly showed that she was mixed with something.

"Hey," Meko replied, rolling her eyes and barely looking in my direction as she moved her round hips and ass like a goddess as she walked to the back of the apartment.

"Come on, y'all. We can go back into my room since my mom has company." Kameko motioned to her friends.

Carmen smiled. "Yeah, as you can see, Kameko's father isn't black, he's Japanese. That heffa in there grew up wanting for nothing. Her father bought her any and everything she asked for. We lived a pretty good lifestyle back then. He was barely home, so I was left home alone with Kameko. Me and Kameko indulged on expensive foods, our home was filled with custom made furniture, and our closets filled with designer labels."

I asked incredulously, with a hint of jealousy, "So what happened? Why are you no longer with her father?" I would never admit it to myself or Carmen, but at that moment, I was jealous of Kameko. Why would Carmen leave me behind to start a new life and give birth to another child that she stayed around to raise?

"I had so much freedom, there was never a dull moment living the life that I once lived. I was blowing through Ken's money like it was water. It came a point when I wasn't even coming home for days. I was out partying doing drugs and drinking, doing whatever I wanted. I didn't care what Ken had to say about anything.

"Ken was an assistant production manager, so he was earning a decent income. I took advantage of all that money until it got out of control. One day Ken came home from work early when he got a phone call from the school saying I wasn't there to pick up Kameko. When he walked in, he found me in the living room with my friends. He caught us mid snort. I loved cocaine and vodka.

"Anyway, he threw my friends out and then beat the shit out of me. One thing led to another, and he threw me out with only the clothes on my back and the shoes on my feet. I couldn't understand how he could throw me away

35

like that, considering I was the mother of his child. I told him that I had no place to stay, but he didn't care."

Listening to Carmen talk non-stop about her 'good life' was making me very emotional. I was hurt, jealous, and angry. I wanted to fight her right there inside that apartment. She was telling me about a man throwing her away, but she didn't give a fuck about how I felt about her throwing me away. We sat there talking for another hour about random things until Carmen finally said she needed to lie down because her body was beginning to ache.

Carmen's words about lying down were meaningless to me at that moment and I found myself concentrating on what I wanted to say.

"I'm mad at you for leaving me. I've always felt alone and confused. But most importantly, I always wanted a mother, and you weren't there for me. Why! Why weren't you there!? Have you ever loved me?" I raised my voice as I began to cry while Carmen nodded without verbally responding. I felt as if a huge weight had lifted off my chest.

Carmen rolled her eyes in my direction, "I know you're mad at me right now, Christian, but what you want me to do about that? I can't change what has already happened." This woman never loved me.

Not the way a mother does her child. She never held me, and from what I remembered, she never even hugged me. I tried to push it all to the back of my mind and focus on Carmen's words, her version of why she walked out of my life.

"You have a lot of nerve to say that to me. Isn't there something more important you're supposed to ask me first? Like how you're leaving made me feel. Carmen, you're the one who makes me feel like I do... no one else, not Kory, my daddy, my kids, not even my uncle Mark, no one but

YOU. You're the one who packed up and left everything behind without even breathing a word to me, your child."

"Christian, what do you want from me? Do I have to continue to answer the same questions? What is so great about getting mad and fighting with me?"

I stared into Carmen's eyes for a moment, seeing the pain she was trying so hard to hide. I was speechless as I sat listening to her bullshit.

"Carmen, tell me whatever you're comfortable telling me. You don't have to tell me everything at once. I know everyone has secrets in their heart they don't like to share, things they try to hide from those around them, and it takes time to open up, but I will get the answers from you that I'm looking for whether it's today, tomorrow, next week, month, or year." Carmen shifted her eyes down to the floor and took a deep breath; she exhaled then stared at me for a moment as if she was unable to speak. Her body

38

trembled slightly, unable to contain its emotion, and tears began to stream down her face.

"Drugs were what I had been doing my entire life even before I met Melvin, but back then, it was prescription drugs. This was long before I began selling my body for money to anyone that wanted it. Christian, I've been raped and partly homeless all because I was addicted to drugs. I was so hooked on heroin. I was almost homeless after Kameko's father stopped giving me money that I was using to help pay the rent. Everybody's not built to handle what life throws at them, but me I managed to make it through." Carmen paused, staring at me like a lost child with nowhere to turn, cold and afraid. Her eyes looked as if they burned from the flow of tears that continued to flow down her face.

I shook my head, hoping that what Carmen was telling me or was about to tell me was the truth. "Wow, that's deep," I responded.

"I was so high on drugs. That was my only will to live. If I hadn't gotten really sick, I would probably still be on the streets or dead."

As hard as I wanted to feel sorry for Carmen, I couldn't. She didn't feel sorry about leaving me. If she would have stayed in Detroit with me and Daddy, then she wouldn't have had such a hard time being pimped out and strung out on drugs.

"Why didn't you get help?" I asked.

"I tried to change my lifestyle many times, and I even tried rehab a couple of times, but I would always end up back on drugs, that's until I became very ill. One day I woke up with salty sweat crawling into and irritating my eyes, my legs were aching, and I could barely get out of bed. I knew it was time I slowed down my lifestyle.

"My health got so bad I could barely walk. That's when I applied for state assistance. No one would hire me because I stayed sick all the time. I applied for disability after talking to the doctors, the state approved me, I get a check each month and a housing allowance that's how I ended up living in this apartment. That's my life, drug addict, prostitute, and now handicapped. I know I wasn't there to help you, but as you can see, I needed someone to help me."

"Why are you trying to avoid talking about why you just up and made the decision to stop being a mother? Carmen, you got yourself together enough to raise Kameko. Do you know what it feels like to hear you talk about the relationship you have with her? So why couldn't you have done the same thing for me? Was I not good enough for you? Did my daddy not treat you like Kameko's daddy did? Was living in Detroit too much for you? Why don't you just admit you love Kameko and don't give a fuck about me?" I yelled, crossing my arms over my chest.

41

"You don't know what you are talking about. Christian, I always loved you, and if I wasn't on drugs, I would have turned over heaven and earth to find you, but I just didn't have the heart to come see you. I was young and dumb back then."

"Damn it, you are really pissing me off. Stop acting like you're a fucking victim! Stop acting like it's not your fault that I feel this way. Don't try to say you love me. That only makes me feel even worse. If you really did love me, you wouldn't have left." I shouted angrily. "Don't you dare tell me you love me again when you don't!" I stood to leave. "It was nice to finally meet you." I made my way toward the front door. I stopped mid-step and turned to face Carmen as she began speaking.

"I know you blame me for everything, and I understand some of it. I hope you'll be able to understand who I am and why I made the decisions I made as well.

After getting your letter, I knew getting you to forgive me would be a long-shot. But you're blaming me for everything, Christian. I don't know how to apologize for all of it, especially the things that happened between you and Mark." I thought all I wanted was to see her hurt, and Carmen's tears did nothing but make me lash out at her more.

"What do you mean you can't apologize for what Mark did to me?" I screamed. "What kind of monster are you? You are worse than Mark! Worse than Mark has ever been to me. What Mark did was wrong, dead wrong, but he never left me. In fact, as twisted as it might seem to you, I know in my heart that Mark loved me."

"But Christian, he was your uncle, and he was older, he knew better. You've forgiven Mark, but you have crucified me. Why can't you forgive me? What do I need to do?" Carmen sobbed.

"First of all, let's get one thing straight, I know what the fuck Mark did to me, I know he was older and my uncle and all that, but you have no right to judge him. I will deal with Mark in my own time, but right now, I am trying to deal with you. You keep trying to remove yourself from all of this, the same way you removed yourself over thirty years ago. This time it's not going to work. You are going to take responsibility for everything bad that has happened to me, beginning with the inappropriate relationship between me and my uncle."

I could have grabbed Carmen by the neck to choke some sense into her I was so mad. I had to calm down or else something bad was going to happen. I hated the woman in front of me more than I have hated anyone else in this world. I took about five deep breaths, a tactic that Dr. Wardelle had taught me in counseling. When I spoke again, I was calmer and quieter, but still as angry as ever.

44

"Carmen, can you put yourself in my place for a minute? Can you imagine still wearing a training bra and having your uncle rubbing on your breasts? I had oral sex before I had a menstrual cramp! Who was I going to tell? My father? What was I supposed to say? That his youngest brother was banging his daughter every chance he got? That was his brother, his baby fucking brother, Carmen. Was I supposed to take the chance that Mark might lie and say I was crazy and making it all up for attention? Guess you forget that my grandmother hated you. There is no way she would have allowed Mark to 'fess up to his predatory ways. I had no one to tell because I should have been able to tell you. That's why I blame YOU." Carmen tilted her head as if she was thinking over what I said.

I inhaled a deep, cool breath and covered my face with my hands for a moment, before mentally scolding myself to get a grip before speaking again.

"You and you alone should have protected me from Mark. Have you ever given any thought to the fact that if you would have been there, I would not have been accessible to Mark? He wouldn't have become my babysitter. That was your damn job. How was I supposed to tell my daddy that I'd become the object of his brother's affection and I liked it?

"Do you know what it's like to live with the guilt of liking, no…loving every single thing about this sick and twisted relationship between me and Mark? You can't tell someone, hey my uncle is molesting me and yes, I like it. You can't say no shit like that, Carmen. So what do you mean that you can't apologize for what Mark did? Why not, you are fuckin' responsible, and I will never forgive you for that!"

I couldn't even look at her anymore. My blood pressure was up, my voice was hoarse, and I was spent.

Whenever I thought about Mark, it took a toll on me emotionally, but facing it in the context of my mother's role in it was more than I could handle. I headed toward the front door for the second time. Carmen's silence spoke volumes and at that moment I wasn't sure if we'd ever speak again.

I hugged Carmen tightly giving her a kiss on the cheek. "I'll come back tomorrow, if that is all right with you?"

"Yes, that's all right with me," Carmen replied.

As I walked out the door, she stood in the doorway watching as I made my way to the car. For a few seconds I felt like we were having a mother daughter moment.

When I returned to the hotel, I took a shower, ordered room service, and called Kory to tell him about my visit with Carmen. We talked for about thirty minutes, I said my good nights to the kids, hung up, and closed my eyes and dreamed of the many possibilities of my relationship with Carmen.

I finally met my mother, I learned I had a younger sister, my grandfather was no longer alive, and Carmen had Multiple Sclerosis, but most importantly, I still didn't have a solid reason why Carmen abandoned me.

Over the course of the week, I spent time with Carmen and Kameko, but Kameko barely spoke to me because she was always on her cell phone gossiping. We strolled up and down Hollywood Boulevard. We went to the Chinese Theatre, Kodak Theatre and the Hollywood Walk of Fame. We took two city tours, shopped on Rodeo Drive, and swam at Venice beach. We ate dinner at the Bubba Gump Shrimp Company, Twenty Five Degrees and Roscoe's Chicken and Waffles. At the end of the week, we went to the swap shops and flea markets on Florence Avenue. I bought Kamryn and the twins clothes from

Baldwin Hills Crenshaw Mall, and I actually witnessed a man selling oranges on the side of the road. I laughed because I had only seen that on television.

My last day in Los Angeles, when I stepped out of my rental car outside of Carmen's apartment, taking in the fresh air, I felt a sickening feeling in my gut as I approached the door. I took a few deep breaths before knocking.

After a few knocks, Carmen opened the door. "Hey, Christian," she said.

"Hey Carmen," I replied as we hugged.

We sat and talked for the better part of thirty minutes about some of the things we did over the past week. Then the room fell silent, and we sat staring at each other for a few seconds.

"I want you to come with me to Detroit for a while. I want to get to know you better," I nervously stated.

During one of our many conversations during the week, I asked Carmen again why she left and never came back. Her response was she didn't want to mess up my life. Then she went on to add that when I was born she wasn't mother material and that she couldn't look after a dog let alone me. But when I tried to force her to give me a more definite answer, she shook her head and said, "I know there's nothing I can say that will change what happened over 30 years ago, so let's leave it alone." I was fuming, but I had to remain calm because I didn't want to lose Carmen again.

"I actually thought about it a few times this week that I should come to Detroit for a visit. Are you sure you want me there?" Carmen asked. She looked as if tears threatened to come, but she swallowed hard, forcing herself not to cry.

"Carmen, lately I haven't been too sure about a lot of

things, but I wouldn't have asked if that's not what I wanted."

I waited for Carmen to say something; she sighed loudly, turned to face me, and placed her hands on her hips. "Christian, I still don't know why you want me there, but I'll go."

I freaked out internally. I didn't know what I wanted to accomplish. Carmen knocked me right out of my thought as she grabbed my hand. "I will go to Detroit. I can't promise how long I will stay, but I will go."

I was very surprised, happy, and confused at the same time. "Okay, I guess you better pack your clothes, get some sleep, and I'll be back to get you in the morning." I walked out the door before Carmen changed her mind.

The next morning, I woke up super early. I looked around my hotel room with a twitching eye; the twitch matched the pulsing of the vein in my forehead. I was afraid of what I could soon be faced with. My cell phone buzzed, causing the whole nightstand to vibrate, and my screen flashed on, informing me that I'd received a voice message. I ignored the missed call once I realized it wasn't from Carmen, and I immediately called her to ensure she was still traveling back to Detroit with me. The previous evening I booked her a one-way airline ticket that set me back almost $800, which included the fee to change my original flight so we could travel together.

I began biting my nails as I sat down on the bed listening to the phone ring. When she answered, I cleared my throat and said, "Good morning."

"Good morning, how are you, Christian?" a soft voice responded on the other end of the phone.

I exhaled all at once, and closed my eyes, trying to calm down for the millionth time. "I'm doing fine. I'm calling to make sure you're still coming home with me." I fiddled with the seam of my pajama top.

"Yes, I'm still going. I just finished packing up the last of my toiletries."

"Okay, I will be there within the next hour or so. We can stop for breakfast before going to the airport." Once Carmen and I ended the call, I jumped in the shower, dressed, grabbed all my bags, utilized the express checkout service, and said my final goodbyes to California.

Once we landed in Detroit, it didn't take long for us to grab our bags and exit off the plane. As we waited by the carousel for our bags, I glanced around at everyone who was waiting. When my eyes spotted Kory, I smiled and waved. Kory and I discussed me wanting to build a relationship with Carmen, but I never called and told him I was actually bringing her to Detroit. Kory was a fusser, he fussed about any and everything, and that's why I never ran anything passed him. I did what I wanted and paid for the consequences of my actions later.

Carmen picked up her bags, and I grabbed my bags and handed my largest suitcase to Kory. He laughed and kissed me on the lips. "I see you surely found time to shop," he said as we walked toward the exit.

"Baby, I would like for you to meet my mother, Carmen. Carmen, this is my husband Kory."

Kory's eyes widened. He quickly reached out and shook her hand. "Hi, nice to meet you," he said, showing all his teeth.

The entire ride home from the airport was pretty much silent. Kory asked Carmen about the flight and living in California, general conversation probably to keep himself from cussing me out.

Kory kept looking at me, giving me the evil eye and shaking his head. I knew he was disgusted with me, but I didn't give a damn. "Have you ever heard the saying it's better to ask for permission than ask for forgiveness?" Kory asked.

"Um, isn't it, it's better to ask forgiveness than permission?" I sarcastically replied.

As Kory pulled the truck into the garage, I sat on the passenger side wishing my babies were home so I could see them, but Kory dropped them off over his mother's house for the night before coming to pick me up from the airport. Once the truck stopped, Kory jumped out, grabbed my luggage and the few bags that Carmen had out of the trunk, and carried them into the house.

"You bring yo' ass back downstairs after you get her settled in," Kory whispered in my ear as I unlocked the backdoor.

"Um huh," I answered him, rolling my eyes, knowing it was about to be some shit.

It was close to midnight, and I was exhausted and wasn't in the mood to hear Kory's shit, but I knew he was not going to let this go...not tonight. I led Carmen upstairs into the guestroom. After showing her where the towels and blankets were, I closed the door behind me, took a deep breath, and walked back down the stairs. I cleared my throat as I walked into the kitchen, noticing Kory sitting at the counter.

He sat there looking frustrated and angry; his deep voice broke the silence in the room. "Christian, why didn't you run this past me before you decided to bring a stranger into our house?" He was so mad that his words started running together.

"Stranger?" That word made me slightly chuckle. "Kory, that's my mother. I spent damn near thirty plus years not having her in my life. You knew this day was coming when I hired the investigator. So what the fuck did you think was going to happen when he found her? Did you really think I was going to leave this alone, that he was going to find her and that was going to be it?"

I knew I was wrong for what I did, but I was going to argue Kory down because I hated being wrong. Yeah, I flew out to California, stayed for a week, called home every day to check on the kids. But I knew where to draw the line, and telling my husband I was bringing my mother back to Detroit never left my lips.

"Please spare me the dramatics, Chris. You know what the hell I'm talking about."

"Naw, I don't, please enlighten me, Mr. Banks, because the shit you talking right now is going into one ear and out the other because she's staying here as long as she wants or until I say she has to leave."

Kory was now standing in my personal space, and it was pissing me off. "What happened to all that shit you were talking about us being a team while we were in counseling? Look how quickly we forget. 'Kory, we need to check with the other person before making major decisions.' I guess that shit only applies when it comes to me. There is no I in team, and there damn sure ain't no Christian in team."

"That's where you're wrong because Kory and Christian Banks make up a team, so there is a Christian in our team."

"Don't get cute, Chris. This is not the time and place. You don't know shit about this woman. You can't find shit out about a person in a week. You told me yourself over the phone she was on drugs."

As the conversation continued, Kory's voice escalated, and it looked like there was no way I was going to be able to avoid having an argument with him after only walking in the house an hour prior. "Kory, don't you think I knew that shit, don't you think I understand she may up and leave again, but I don't care what you, yo' mama, my daddy, Aunt Whit, Kameko, or even Carmen says, I deserve to know who my mother is, and I damn sure deserve to know why she left me."

I now had tears in my eyes. I was tired from the six-hour plane ride from California, and I had a lot of questions running through my mind, and I felt like if I couldn't depend on anyone else I at least deserved the support of my husband, damn.

"Chris, she gone clip our shit, all crack heads are thieves. I hustled for damn near ten years back in the day. I sold to all walks of life, so I know how them muthafuckn' crack heads operate. They're sneaky and can't be trusted. I don't give a damn how you feel about her being here, but a current or ex-crack head staying in my house with my family is not the move."

I stopped in my tracks and glared at Kory like he was crazy; my little trip upstairs to take a bath was being put on the back burner because Kory would not leave this shit alone. "Damn, can't we pick this up in the morning? I'm tired. I've been up all day. My flight was six hours long, now you want to argue?" Every inch I took closer to the stairs, Kory moved an inch closer to me and was now right on the heels of my feet. "Listen, K-Boy, the decisions I make concerning my mother are my problem, not yours."

"Chris, don't do this, not tonight. Don't act like I have not supported you every step of the way in helping you find your mother. You know it has nothing to do with that. My problem is you should have discussed this with me, your *husband*. I should have been consulted about your decision to bring Carmen to Detroit. Why the fuck do you think it was okay to surprise me with this shit at the airport? But you know what? You knew exactly what you were doing."

"Thank you, Mr. Kory, for giving me permission, but guess what? I don't give a damn. She's not leaving here until I find out why the hell she bailed out on me. Got it? Good, now good night." I didn't even wait around for him to answer. As I walked up the stairs, I heard the garage door open and the back door slam, and a few minutes later, Kory's truck was peeling out the driveway.

Next Morning

I was washing the dishes when I heard Carmen tiptoe into the kitchen. "Christian, would it be better if I just left? Would you feel better if I was just back in California?" I couldn't believe what she was saying to me. Before I knew it, I had wrapped my wet, soapy hands around her neck.

As I knocked her down onto my new kitchen floor, I yelled as if I was possessed, "Bitch, you are the reason for everything that has happened to me, and all you can think to

61

say is should you leave again? Is that your fuckin' answer to everything, just to leave? Huh?" I must have repeated those lines over and over again because the next thing I knew, Kory and Kamryn were prying my fingers from around the neck of the woman that gave birth to me. The twins, Kylie and Klarke were screaming in the background. I just kept hearing Kory yelling, "What the fuck, what, the fuck?"

When they finally separated us, I stormed out of the kitchen. At that time, I didn't care that Kory was fuming, my babies were scared, or that my mother was gasping for air. I stomped out on the patio and slammed the patio door. I hoped that this would alert everyone in that house not to fuck with me! No such luck.

Here comes Kory. Oh God, he knows me well enough, why won't he leave me alone? Here goes the bullshit.

"Christian, what was *that*?" he asked.

I shook my head, again hoping he'd get the message, but I knew Kory better than that; he was not leaving.

"Christian, besides your father, I think I know you better than anybody in this world, and I walked in on you strangling your mother, the one that you went through hell to find. So now that you have this woman in the house that I pay the mortgage on, with kids that I support living with me, and the woman that I love more than life, you are going to tell me what the fuck just happened or that little episode between you and Carmen will be only the beginning of the hell that is about to break loose in this house. Now start talking, damn it!"

"Kory, I snapped! I'll be damned if I let that woman make me feel like I have to walk on egg shells in my own fucking home. She abandoned me, and her solution to everything is RUN. Instead of her facing our problem like a real woman, the first thing that comes out of her mouth is do

I want her to go back to California. What the fuck, I'm trying to get my life together not have it torn apart all over again." I was angry; everything that had happened between me and Carmen was crashing down on me too fast, too hard.

"I'm a very important part of this household. Chris, I'm letting you know right now, if I come home or witness another episode like what I walked in on, neither one of you will have the chance to decide if she's going back to Cali because I will have her on a plane so fast she won't know what hit her. And I mean that. This shit has to stop."

I nodded in agreement; I didn't want to waste anymore of my time and energy discussing this with Kory.

CHAPTER 3

I could tell that Dr. Wardelle was waiting anxiously for me when I came in for my appointment. Sometimes I questioned why I continued to see him. At first, I admit, I didn't think this counseling thing was going to work and had no problem saying so. I admit that I was wrong because this man single-handedly saved my marriage. I have always loved Kory, but there was a time when I didn't like him, and I didn't think love was enough to save us. Losing KJ allowed me to do what I had wanted to do for a long time, just fade away. I didn't love myself anymore, and even though I loved Kory, I didn't want to and I wanted him to stop loving me.

Dr. Wardelle helped us deal with grief, infidelity, and communication and trust issues. He helped me to see that my biggest problem was not knowing what to do with the feelings that I had. Like the feelings I had for Carmen, Mark, Kory, Kamryn, all that. I was just lashing out. He helped to figure that out. No one had ever been able to do that. I told this man more about me than I had told anyone, including Kory and my daddy. He helped me to begin to feel good about being Christian. I grew up my entire life being ashamed of who I was. Every single one of my friends had a mother. Some had mothers, step-mothers, god-mothers, grandmothers, all of that. I didn't have shit. I couldn't appreciate what Mel tried to give me because I was so consumed with what I didn't have.

People used to always tell me that life could be worse. But not to me. I felt like I was living in hell. But the day I lost my son, my child, my everything... that day. That was the day I realized that life could get worse. But Dr. Wardelle told me I had two options: either get my life in order before it got worse or wallow in my grief and allow KJ's tragedy to send me on a downward spiral until I hit rock fucking bottom. I didn't know much, but I did know this, if losing KJ was not rock bottom, then I didn't want to find out what was.

So while I was scheduling my kids' dentist appointments, my massage appointments, and oil changes for our cars, I was also diligent in scheduling my time with Dr. Wardelle. Although I was now a bit apprehensive about meeting with him because I knew Kory had called and told him about my fight with Carmen and Kory's so dramatic, I knew he probably told this man that I tried to kill Carmen or something. Kory didn't see Dr. Wardelle anymore, but he too was grateful for the way Dr. Wardelle worked with us through our bullshit, and any time Kory thought I might be 'falling off,' he was quick to call Dr. Wardelle and let him know. I guess he was afraid I might not 'fess up to wrapping my fingers around my mother's throat.

"Hi Christian," Dr. Wardelle said with a smirk on his face. I already felt ashamed. Like a little girl being called into the principal's office.

"Hello," I said while rolling my eyes at no one in particular.

"How are you, Christian, how have you been?" he asked sarcastically.

"Well, it's been a rough couple of days."

"Tell me about it, Christian. Tell me about your week."

"Did Kory call you?" I asked him to see what he would say because I knew my husband and I knew he called him. He was such a tattletale.

"Yes, he did, you know Mr. Banks," he said with a smile. "But I want to hear it from you. What happened to set you off?"

There was something about being in the presence of Dr. Wardelle that made me so vulnerable. I started to cry before I even began to speak. When I composed myself a bit, I said, "She, she, she…" damn, it wouldn't come out. "Dr. Wardelle, she asked me should she leave," I was finally able to say. "After all I did to find her and get her here."

Dr. Wardelle slowly nodded, but I could tell that he wasn't letting me off the hook. "Christian, while I understand that Carmen talking about leaving upset you, I know you well enough to know that there is more to it than her just threatening to leave. Carmen coming here to Michigan was never supposed to be permanent, was it?" Dr. Wardelle already knew the answer because we'd discussed this very thing in sessions months ago when I mentioned to him I was reaching out to Carmen, so I shook my head no, feeling like a little child being scolded.

"But, she's not sorry," I said while continuing to shake my head. "I think I expected her to be sympathetic, you know? I expected her to wrap her arms around me and tell me how she would do anything to make it up to me. I thought she would tell me how horrible she feels for leaving me the way she did. I wanted her to tell me that she knows it's her fault that me and Mark...you know.

"I wanted her to say bad things about my grandmother for being so evil to me and allowing Mark to use me for his pleasure. I wanted so much from Carmen, and she's not even sorry." I was beyond sobbing now. I had given up on wiping my face. I could see the mascara running. I felt so weak, but I continued. "How could she look me in my face after all these years, Dr. Wardelle, and tell me, her first born child that she abandoned, that she doesn't know how to apologize?" I was basically moaning my words now. I had to stop because my nose was running now. I had completely fallen apart within a mere five minutes of being in my counselor's office.

"Christian," he said sympathetically, "we talked about this at great length when you first began coming back to see me. Remember? We talked about your mother and the fact that you knew very little about her. I warned you against forming any expectations. We really couldn't make any predictions about how she'd respond to your request to build a relationship with her.

"Remember, she didn't respond when you first contacted her. I specifically asked you if you were ready for the possibility that she wouldn't want a relationship with you. You kept pushing, and both Kory and I were deeply concerned that this would happen. Do you remember?"

Everything he said was true. He warned me. Kory warned me. Mel warned me. Marcella warned me. They all did. I nodded and said, "Yes, I remember. But, I couldn't imagine her not being sorry. I heard everything that you all were saying about Carmen." I was shaking my head while thinking at how things had turned out.

"I know you all can't understand. You all had mothers who loved you like a mother should. Take Kory, for example. His mother worships him."

I don't speak too much about Leslie, but she couldn't fathom a life without her children. She gave everything she had when raising them. I don't like Mama Lez, that's no secret, but some of it's because I'm jealous. I want a mother to love me like she loves her kids. I want a mother to cook dinner and call and beg me to come over and eat.

"Hell, there were times when I would have just finished preparing dinner, and Kory would still go over to his mother's just because. If he wouldn't go over there, she'd make Phil bring her to our house. Not to visit mind you, just to drop off the food. She really just wanted to see Kory's face. Kory is a grown ass man, but his mother still wants to see his face!

"And this woman who carried me in her womb is already tired of looking at my face after two damn seconds? Why? Why? Why doesn't my mother love me, Dr. Wardelle? What was so wrong with me? How could every child I ever came into contact with have a mother except me?"

I was just too through now, and although Dr. Wardelle had become engrossed in our lives over the years, this was the first time I actually saw him shed tears. Dr. Wardelle felt my pain, but he didn't have an answer to my question. He didn't know why Carmen didn't love me.

He finally said, "Christian, you wanted a happy fairy tale ending to what you consider to be your horror film. If simply finding her was what you wanted, then locating her would have been enough for you. You weren't honest with yourself or your expectations and that, Mrs. Banks, is why you attacked Carmen." I hated when he called me Mrs. Banks. When he called me Christian, I felt like we were friends, but when he called me Mrs. Banks, it seemed so cold and impersonal.

"Say what you want, Doc, but I told her detail after detail of the pain that I have suffered at the hands of so many and the only thing she can think of to say is should she leave. What kind of thing is that to ask me? I paid an astronomical amount of money to find her. She never tried to find me. I traveled across the country to get her. I paid for her to come here so we could get to know one another.

"I went against not only my father's but my husband's wishes as well and still brought her here. I allowed her into our lives, and she wants to know if she should leave? My uncle... you know... for years," I said sobbing uncontrollably, "and she's not sorry about that? If that's expecting too much from the woman that brought me into this world, then oh fucking well!"

I got up and walked to the window. I was mad at Dr. Wardelle right now. I wanted to leave. I turned back, retrieved my purse, and walked out of the office.

As I walked swiftly to the elevator, my phone rang, I was crying so I couldn't see the number, "Christian, I am sorry if I upset you." It was Dr. Wardelle. "You know that sometimes the truth hurts. We can refrain from discussing Carmen any further today, but if you have time, I would like you to return to my office. I have something I would like to run by you. If not, it's okay, I will see you next month, and we can discuss it at that time."

As much as I wanted to leave, I wanted to know what he wanted to discuss with me, especially since he said it didn't have anything to do with Carmen. So, I turned around and walked slowly back to his office. As I sat down, he said, "Remember when you gave me permission to contact Mark to inquire about attending a counseling session with us?" he asked. I remembered us talking about it. I told him that I wasn't going to be the one to suggest it to Mark. I didn't have a real reason for not doing it. I just didn't want to do it. Dr. Wardelle asked for my permission to call Mark. He said that Mark might be more agreeable to it if he called him anyway. I wasn't sure about it at first, but told him that I would think about it. After a few sessions of him asking me, I finally gave in and provided him with Mark's phone number. Now that he was bringing it up again, my stomach was in knots.

"Yes, I remember, but you also said you would do it in time."

"Well, I called him," he said so matter of fact.

"And?" I raised my eyebrow as my stomach did a hula hoop dance.

"He sounded reluctant at first, but when I started telling him that you and I had discussed your *relationship* in our sessions, he asked me if he was going to prison. He sounded more scared than anything. I reassured him that I was not a legal authority and had no intention on filing any legal action against him. He quickly told me that he would come in. I assume he wasn't comfortable with the phone discussion anymore."

"So," I said, a bit confused. "Mark has been here?" I asked.

"No, but I would like to schedule a meeting with the three of us. Honestly, Christian, I really don't think you are going to get to the bottom of your unhappiness until you deal with your issues involving Mark," he said for about the hundredth time since we began meeting alone.

"Dr. Wardelle, I know you think Mark is the cause of my problems, but I don't. My problems are because Carmen abandoned me. I really don't want to drag my uncle into this. I am trying to forget about this *thing* with Mark. The fact that I have spoken about it more times than I can count over the last year between discussing it with you and discussing it with Carmen makes me uncomfortable. No one can ever know about this.   "Most things don't bother me in the least, but blowing the whistle on me and Mark's thing is enough to make me consider suicide. Seriously. I know you don't understand it, no one does, but I still love my uncle, and I don't want him in jail, I don't want him to lose his job or his family, I don't want the be the cause of anyone else's pain, and if this thing gets out, that's exactly what will happen."

"Christian, no one will know about Mark and you. This is between the people that you want it to be between, but you have to deal with this or else you are going to continue down the road of self-destruction. I can see that you really love Mark. And you might not think that I don't understand it, but I have counseled several incest abuse victims. I understand more than you think. I don't want to judge Mark, that's not my place.

"I want him to help you understand how and why your relationship progressed the way it did. You need to hear him say it. He needs to know that he still has a very strong hold on you. You have said more than once that your husband and children deserve more. You can't give them more if you don't adequately deal with your unresolved feelings for your uncle. My guess is that he needs to do the same."

I just took a deep breath. I mean, what was I supposed to say? I came in here trying to defend myself about choking the shit out of my mother and now here I was contemplating being in the same room with Mark and talking about years of inappropriate sexual contact between us.

"Christian, I see your apprehension. Tell me this, when was the last time you saw your uncle?"

I had to think for a minute. "Oh, I saw him at my grandfather's birthday party a few months ago." I knew what was coming next, so I answered before he could ask. "No, we didn't have sex. I told you we haven't had sex since before KJ. Remember?"

"Christian, I know what you told me. But I also know that you still have feelings for Mark that have not been dealt with. So tell me about your grandfather's party," he said in almost a demanding tone.

"What about it? I was there, Mark was there, no big deal," I said and I meant it. It really was no big deal.

"Did you two talk?"

"I mean, small talk. He asked me how everything was going, I asked him the same. He said my kids were cute, I said his were grown, you know stuff like that."

"At this party, were you ever alone with Mark?"

"No, we were always in the company of others."

"That's what I mean, Christian. Why can't you be alone in the same room with Mark? It's not normal for an uncle and his niece to avoid being alone. You and Mark are not comfortable being alone because you don't trust yourselves. When was the last time you were alone with Mark?"

I had to think hard. I couldn't remember, and I really couldn't think straight because I was pondering what Dr. Wardelle had said about us not being able to be alone with one another. "I don't know, Doc, a few months before my grandfather's party, so about a year ago I guess. My grandfather had fallen and broken his hip. Mark and I ran into one another then."

"What happened? If your grandfather was around, then you weren't alone, right?"

"My grandfather was taking tests or x-rays or something, and I was waiting for him to come back to the room to say goodbye. Mark came in expecting me to be gone already, and we both waited for my granddad to return. But we weren't alone for long, ten to fifteen minutes tops." I didn't know why he couldn't leave this alone. I told him that Mark and I had been over for years, damn.

"What happened, Christian? What happened when you and Mark waited alone for your grandfather?" he asked accusingly. "Did you and Mark do anything inappropriate?"

I sat there quietly. As I tried to remember that day, I did remember Mark hugging me as he walked in. But that was normal, wasn't it? I'd seen plenty of uncles hug their nieces. Hell, I hugged all of my uncles every time I saw them. There's nothing wrong with that. But I guess it's not normal for that uncle to use his hands to quickly explore his niece's body, the parts of her body that should only be caressed by his niece's husband. I guess it's not normal for him to plant kisses on his niece's neck when clearly her cheek was in plain view.

I guess it's not normal for him to whisper in his niece's ear that her husband was one lucky man. I guess it's also not normal for his niece to break the embrace after feeling a hard-on pressing into her abdomen, and I guess it's abnormal as hell for his niece to walk to her car reading a text message from him that read *Every time I make love to my wife, I think of you.* Hell naw, this shit wasn't normal, and situations like the one in my grandfather's hospital room had happened one too many times. Dr. Wardelle was right. Although Mark and I had not loved one another since I became pregnant with KJ, we had been more than inappropriate over the years. So I finally spoke up and decided against telling him what happened in my grandfather's room and simply said, "Okay, schedule the appointment."

CHAPTER 4

My cell phone was ringing before eight on a Sunday morning. I always felt it was beyond rude to call someone on a Sunday before nine unless it's an emergency. Which explains my rush to answer the phone before the annoying ringing woke up Kory. Unfortunately while I was rushing to answer the phone, it stopped ringing but that didn't stop me from hitting my toe on the edge of the bed. I looked at my cell phone and didn't recognize the number from the missed call; I sighed then cursed when my phone started ringing again. I growled into the phone, "This better be an emergency."

"Hey, this Kameko." I could tell by her dry and aggressive tone that she was about to start some shit. I didn't get a good vibe from her when we first met in California, and it seemed like her attitude toward me hadn't changed.

"Hey Kameko, what's up?" I spoke as I walked down the stairs toward the kitchen.

"It's been a little over four months, so your bonding time is over. Send Mama home where she belongs."

"Excuse me!" I raised my voice as I digested her words. This bitch was trying to give me a run for my money, but I wasn't going to allow that shit to fly. No one told me what to do.

"You heard me, so there is no need to repeat myself."

I was speechless for about thirty seconds. I couldn't get with this chick; for the life of me, I didn't understand why as sisters we couldn't get off on the right foot.

"It's too early in the morning for this, so I'ma need you to bring your tone down about five pitches," I politely expressed.

"I'm not trying to hear all of that."

"Kameko, what is it that you really want because calling my phone with an attitude is not working."

When Kameko spoke again, her tone was softer, but still harsh. "If you must know, we're being evicted in ten days if the rent is not paid. The landlord placed a noticed on the door I guess this morning."

"Why don't you get a job? That way you will be able to pay the rent yourself, or better yet, why don't you get your daddy to pay for it. He's rich, isn't he?" I sarcastically asked.

Kameko defensively responded, "This isn't his problem, and for the record, I have a job, we were doing fine until you came around."

"So what you're saying is that you live off Carmen's disability check every month?" I could tell by all the huffing and puffing she was doing through the phone that she wasn't liking my line of questioning, but I wasn't going to allow this broad to dial my phone and then proceed to tell me what I was going to do and not do.

"No! We help each other out. I don't have to explain nothing to you. Put my mother on a plane today, or I will call the police and tell them you kidnapped her, or I will do one better, I will get in touch with your husband and tell him how trifling you are."

This bitch was talking reckless to me. Who in the hell did she think she was calling me trifling? I was going to call her bluff on this one because there wasn't shit she could tell Kory about me because she didn't know shit about me. "Okay, call him, I don't give a damn, but it's going to be a waste of time."

"Are you sure about that because I know I wouldn't want my husband to know that I was fucking my uncle and was getting pleasure out of it." She chuckled.

Suddenly beads of perspiration began forming on my forehead. I damn near dropped my cell phone. My mouth was wide open, and this bitch had me speechless once again. How in the fuck did she know about Mark? I knew my past was going to come back to haunt me; karma is a bitch. Carmen, must have let her read my letter, so I guess she really didn't give a fuck about me. That was personal information that I shared with Carmen, and that letter was for her eyes only.

"Listen, Kameko, I've been really patient with you, but you're about to make me go there. Don't you ever call my phone and threaten me with what you think you know about me. You don't know shit about me. You don't know what I've been through in my life.

"I grew up without my mother, and all I've been trying to do is build a relationship with her and possibly with you. If this was about money, then you should have said that, but don't call me telling me what I'm going to do."

This chick actually had me nervous. I didn't care if I had to pay this bitch's rent until the end of time, Kory was never to find that shit out. As soon as we ended this call, I would be talking to Carmen about this; she either ran her mouth about my business or she left my damn letter lying around. Whichever one it was, I wasn't going to let that shit slide.

Kameko sighed as if she was trying to keep her frustration down; she took a deep breath before she began speaking. "Bullshit! Who are you to tell me about what you've been through in life? I don't give a fuck. I lived with a drug addict, grew up listening to gunshots at all times of the day, people fighting and screaming up and down the street. Stepped over homeless people scattered on the sidewalk and junkies passed out as I walked to and from school. Gang's rule and drug activity happened right in my face." Kameko paused for a moment and then spoke again. "So, Ms. Christian, I made the best out of what I had exactly like you did."

My whole body felt cold as she spoke; I actually felt bad for her. It seemed as if she was hurting as much as I was, but for different reasons. I hated to give in, but I had to send Kameko the money to get her off my back. She did have one thing right; I didn't know her, and based on the life she's living, I wouldn't put it past someone in her situation to do what they felt necessary to make others feel the pain she was feeling. In Kameko's situation, the pain reliever she was using against me was calling Kory.

I quickly changed the subject because this conversation was going down the wrong path. Taking deep breaths, I asked "How much is the rent?" By this time I was in the kitchen whispering, so Kory wouldn't overhear our conversation.

"Twelve hundred."

"Twelve hundred, are you serious?" I quickly retorted. "That's a lot of money." That shit they lived in was one blow from being condemned. I wouldn't be caught dead living in that place.

"Well that's how much it is, and it needs to be paid this week, and they will only take cash."

I stared at kitchen floor with my eyebrows raised. Well I'll be damn; I didn't know how to respond.

"I'll Western Union the money tomorrow because I don't have access to that type of cash today."

"All right," Kameko answered without saying thank you.

"How do you spell your name?"

"K A M E K O, last name Johnson."

When she said that, I …my heart dropped. Carmen had a lot of damn nerve. She was way beyond disrespectful with this one. She left me behind and then up and gave the child that she had with some unknown man my daddy's last name.

"I will call you tomorrow after I send the money, oh and one more thing, Carmen will be staying with me a little longer, so don't you ever call my phone threatening me. Have a good day." I ended the call and closed my cell phone before Kameko could respond.

One hour later

"Good morning, Christian," Carmen spoke, startling me; I must have been day dreaming because I never heard her walk in the kitchen. It all worked out because this gave me the opportunity to talk to her alone. There were things

93

we needed to get straight without Kory or the kids over hearing.

"Good morning. I received a phone call from Kameko this morning. Do you know anything about that?" I immediately looked Carmen directly in her face; my daddy always told me that a person's body language determines if they're telling the truth or lying. And based on Carmen's current nervous actions, she knew it wasn't a good conversation.

Carmen looked at me curiously for a moment. "She did? Well, she called my phone yesterday asking for your and Kory's cell phone numbers. She told me she wanted to call and get to know you two."

I cocked my head at her. "Is that so? Because when she called me this morning, she didn't sound like she wanted to get to know me. She was actually calling to blackmail me

94

if I didn't send you back to California or send her rent money. By the way, how much is the rent?"

"With the past due amount that's owed, I think it's around twelve hundred." I wanted to laugh at Carmen. This game she and Kameko were trying to run on me was hilarious, and they had this shit to the penny.

"So I guess I can't trust you? I wrote you a letter pouring out my personal thoughts and experiences, and you go and share that shit with Kameko, and now she's calling me threatening to call Kory with information I shared with you." By this time I didn't care who was woke or who overheard this conversation because in the back of my mind contacting Carmen was turning out to be a decision I was regretting.

She shuddered, not out of fear. "Christian, I didn't tell Meko anything, so don't accuse me of something I didn't do. I left the letter in California, so she must have found it."

"So Carmen, what do you think is wrong? Why would Kameko try to blackmail me?" I didn't expect an answer from her; I was asking to get under her skin.

"I don't know, Christian, and I want you to believe me when I say I don't have anything to do with whatever Kameko is up to."

"But you did know she was going to call me, and you couldn't give me the heads up. Are you playing favoritism? Damn, can't you look out for me just once? How many times do I have to ask you that? I feel like I'm begging you to be a part of my life."

"Christian, take a good look at my life. I'm not in the position to play favoritism with anyone. I don't have myself together. How do you expect me to look out for someone else?"

Carmen was pushing my buttons, and on top of everything, she was starting to raise her voice at me, and no one including my own husband was going to disrespect me inside my own house.

"Well, you need to get on the phone with YOUR daughter and let her know I'm not about to play these little games with her. Nothing or nobody will come between me and my family. Kory is to never find out about this. I will take ALL the necessary measures to protect my family." I was so close in Carmen's face that I'm almost sure she smelled the peppermint tea I drank an hour earlier.

"Christian, I'm not getting in the middle of that. If there is something you want to say to Meko, you need to tell her yourself. I'm not about to pick sides."

"Carmen, I'm not asking you to pick sides, I've fought many battles, but what I need you to do is warn your Kameko not to play with fire because she will get burned." Carmen shook her head as if she was listening, but I don't think she gave a fuck about what I was saying. We sat in silence for a few moments, a few moments turned into a few more minutes before Carmen finally spoke. She looked me directly in the eyes for the first time since we met.

"Christian, this is not going to be easy for me to explain, but I went from loving you but feeling overwhelmed to being a damned good mother at times," Carmen said quickly taking the conversation off Kameko. "Melvin had plenty of help from his mother and Whitney. I had no one. I felt like I was living in a foreign country where I didn't even speak the language."

"But it was neither my grandmother nor Aunt Whit's responsibility to take care of me."

Carmen continued talking as if she hadn't heard me. "When I first left, I would ask myself the same questions over and over. How could I leave my child? How could I be the mother who walks away?"

"Oh really, so what answers did you come up with?" I sarcastically asked.

With hesitation in her tone, she replied, "I never came up with an answer. I was in mommy shock without a strong marriage to support me. My marriage was failing. Melvin was never home, yet he was the one who wanted a family. He begged me to keep you when I found out I was pregnant. He promised to take care of everything." I watched Carmen's body language. I could smell bullshit a mile away, and there was no doubt in my mind that she was being a drama queen. "It raised a little issue for me that I neglected to mention to anyone I never wanted to be a mother.

"Christian, I had no idea what to do with you. Even feeding you and changing your diaper was a challenge. I was afraid of being overwhelmed, of being exhausted, or of opening my eyes one day and realizing I had lost myself and my life was over. I was never a mother in anything but name." Carmen wiped a stray tear from her cheek.

"But..." I began but was interrupted by the voice from the doorway.

Our conversation was cut short when Kory walked into the kitchen. "Good morning, ladies." He looked at me and then at Carmen as if he could feel the tension in the room.

"Good morning," we replied in unison. I couldn't tell which one of our responses was the driest.

"I looked in on Kamryn and the twins before I came down. All three were spread out all over their beds, covers were on the floor, and legs and arms were hanging off the bed. They were knocked out cold." Kory was trying to warm up the ice cold scene inside the kitchen. "You all right?" He walked up and whispered in my ear.

I didn't even respond. I nodded and walked out the kitchen. As I was leaving, Kory's cell phone began buzzing. I overheard him talking. At first I thought it was someone calling to make a Monday appointment, but oh, how wrong was I.

"Hey Kameko, how are you?" I heard Kory speak. I inhaled deeply, and my anger completely escaped me. This bitch was really out to get me; she didn't even give me a chance to send the money, and now she was on the phone with my husband. I stood outside the kitchen, listening to Kory laughing on the phone with Kameko for about five minutes "Well, I appreciate you calling, and I look forward to meeting you soon."

"Who was that?" I asked, pretending to walk back into the kitchen, knowing damn well I knew exactly who was on the phone. Carmen didn't say a word; she sat at the kitchen counter, flipping through a magazine as if she wasn't even in the room. I did notice her glancing up when I asked Kory who he was talking to. I didn't know if she thought Kory was going to lie to me or if I was going to go the fuck off on Kory, her, and Kameko.

"Kameko, she said she wanted to keep in touch and that she talked to you already this morning, but she didn't want us to think she didn't care." It was time I pulled some tricks out my bag for this wench because she was playing with fire and I never lose.

Two seconds later, my cell phone started to vibrate. I grabbed my phone and left the room after seeing it was Kameko calling. My knees buckled as I walked outside for a little privacy.

"What the fuck is your problem? What did you tell him?" I was so angry that steam was probably blowing from my hair.

"I didn't tell him shit, but I wanted you to know that I'm not playing, and if you don't pay this rent, the next conversation I have with Kory will be very deep and informative." This time Kameko hung up on me before I could respond.

CHAPTER 5

I was so nervous leading up to my appointment with Dr. Wardelle and Mark; I didn't know what to do. I woke up extra early. I made love to my husband extra hard. That always satisfied him. Especially since I also cooked a big breakfast and served it to him in bed, too. I was on a roll. I was even nice to Carmen. She too was served breakfast in bed, and that is something that I never did. I felt no need to serve the woman who hadn't found the words to apologize to me for... forget it; it's not worth the effort. I was tired of re-hashing why she'd always be on my shit list. I also knew that she wasn't feeling well, so instead of having Carmen find her own way to her doctor's appointment that afternoon, I called and ordered a car service to take her, and I paid for it. I knew going to the doctor for her MS took a toll on her.

I changed my clothes seven times and styled my hair five different ways. My perfume, make up, the purse I was carrying, all became such a huge deal. I was literally a nervous wreck trying to get ready for this appointment. It could have only been about seeing Mark because I saw Dr. Wardelle every four weeks. I tried to remind myself that I'd divulged almost everything to him, but there was no telling what would come out today. I wasn't sure how honest Mark was willing to be. I wasn't sure how honest I was going to continue to be now that the session included Mark. This whole thing with Mark was something that I swore I would keep to myself and knowing that Carmen and Dr. Wardelle knew made me extremely uneasy.

I hadn't seen Mark in a minute, but that quickly came to an end because as fate would have it, we pulled up in the parking garage at exactly the same time. My heart beat a rhythm it never had before. Maybe I should stay in the car and wait until he went in. I was about 20 minutes early anyway. I saw him getting out. I hoped he didn't stop at my truck. I hurried and pulled out my cell phone, but I couldn't dial the number of any of my contacts fast enough because Mark began knocking on my passenger side window. I simply put the phone back in my purse and unlocked the door.

"Hi Christian, you look nice," he said nervously. He was staring at me.

"Thanks," I said, immediately feeling uncomfortable.

"Look,", Mark said, "I tried calling you a few times because I wanted to talk to you first before the session, but you never called back."

106

He was still staring at me. I was tongue tied all of a sudden. But finally I responded, "I've been busy. You know my mother, well, Carmen is here. I have three small children, a business to run, and a husband to please." I don't know why I said that part about my husband and kids because I knew darn well that Mark knew I had a family. I guess I needed to reassure myself.

"I know, baby girl," he said. Calling me baby girl was something that I hated and loved at the same time. My face must have told the story because he jumped in apologetically and said, "I wasn't trying to upset you. I know you've been busy. I'm sorry. I'm rambling. I am really nervous about being here. I was totally surprised when your counselor called. I am not sure why because I sort of thought that...you know...might come up in your sessions. I have been a nervous fool." He hesitated before speaking again. "What all did you tell him?"

"Everything," I said. "Everything that I could remember." Mark went limp in the seat.

"I was afraid of that. I don't want to sound insensitive, but I have to ask you if there is any way I can go to jail behind this. I have been scared to death of that. I asked your counselor the same thing, and he said no. But I want to be sure."

Of course I had already thought about that and discussed it with Dr. Wardelle. "No, Mark," I said. "This is about me trying to get past all of this." I said with my hands in the air as if "this" was something he could see. "I need to move on with my life." Here came the tears.

"Mark, I don't know why we do what we do." I looked at him like he had an answer for me. He was quiet. No answer. "I'm so confused. I want to get past this." Again, my hands air quoted. Somehow I guess "this" was connected to my hands. I wanted to throw whatever "this" was away, skip the appointment, get Mark out of my car, and go home to live a normal life. But "this" was too much. I was starting to doubt that I would ever be normal. The real question was how long I would be able to continue a façade of being normal.

"I want us to be like regular uncles and nieces. I want to be normal. That's it. This includes no jail time, Mark, no big reveal to everyone, no telling Mel, no calling Jasmine and damn sure, no calling Kory. This is about getting to the bottom of us and this thing we have. That's it, Mark. That's it."

I could tell he was surprised to hear me speak so passionately about our thing because after all these years, we'd never talked about it. We sat in silence for a moment and then the weirdest thing happened. It made me think back to Dr. Wardelle's comment about me and Mark not being able to be alone with one another. Mark reached over to hug me. I guess it would be okay, so I sort of leaned in to hug him back. I smelled the same familiar scent that he'd worn for years, the scent that I absolutely forbade Kory from buying. Suddenly, I became stiff. He wasn't even trying anything, but I was afraid for him to hug me.

I couldn't relax, and Mark noticed. He backed away, throwing his hands in the air in a way that I could see he wasn't trying anything. I felt bad. This was what I had to stop doing. I had to stop feeling bad. Mark got out of the car. I thought I hurt his feelings. He came around and opened my door. He had this pitiful look on his face. I didn't know why, but I turned around and hugged him.

It was an awkward hug. The kind that two former lovers do when they run into one another years after they've gone their separate ways. The kind that's not sexual per se, but far from friendly. Not the kind of hug you give your parent, but less affectionate than the one you give your spouse. The kind where you aren't sure what will happen when the embrace is broken. The kind that I shouldn't be having in this parking garage with my uncle.

"I love you, baby girl," he whispered as we let go. "I mean that, Christian, I love you." I don't know if it was appropriate or not, but I liked hearing it. Nothing more was said as we walked silently through the garage into the building where Dr. Wardelle's office was located, but it was obvious that both of us were on edge.

"Good morning, Mr. Johnson," Dr. Wardelle said as he reached out to shake Mark's hand.

"Good morning, Dr. Wardelle," Mark said. He was able to get it out, but he was nervous. I could tell. His palms were so sweaty that he actually wiped them on his pants before shaking Dr. Wardelle's hand.

As soon as I was about to have a seat, Dr. Wardelle asked me to wait in the lobby for a few minutes. He said something about wanting to talk to Mark alone. This made me uneasy. What were they about to say about me that I couldn't hear? After about twenty minutes, Dr. Wardelle's administrative assistant told me they were ready for me to re-join the session. When I walked in, I could see that Mark was sweating profusely. He looked like he'd been in a fight. I was more curious than ever to know what that little private meeting was about.

"Christian and Mark, I really appreciate you agreeing to group therapy. Christian, I know you weren't a fan of any type of therapy for quite some time and only attended out of obligation. Mark, I know that you were sort of blindsided by the idea of therapy and discussing your relationship with Mrs. Banks. A few months ago, Christian opened up about a relationship that you two formed while teenagers. She told me that you are her uncle, her father's youngest brother and that most of your activity during your teen years took place at the home of your parents, Mr. Johnson. It is also my understanding that this relationship really has yet to end." Dr. Wardelle spoke as if he was reading and indictment or something.

I jumped right in, "No, the relationship is over, Dr. Wardelle. Mark and I have not been together in years. Our relationship is most definitely over."

Dr. Wardelle looked at Mark for approval, "Is this true, Mark, has the relationship you formed with Christian come to a close? Did it end years ago as Christian stated?"

"No," Mark said quietly.

"No?" I said loudly, looking Mark dead in the face. "Mark, you and I haven't had sex in years, and you know it. Don't come in here lying to my counselor." I couldn't believe this Negro. Mark had never turned on me in my thirty something years on this earth, and now he chose to lie. I was heated, and it was showing. Dr. Wardelle asked me to calm down. He reminded me that this was going to be uncomfortable.

"Mark, why is it that you think you and Christian have a difference of opinions as to when the relationship ended?" Dr. Wardelle asked Mark. Again, I jumped in before Mark could lie anymore.

"Why are we talking about this?" I said with the most twisted look on my face that I could make. "Shouldn't you be asking him why he started touching me in the first place? Shouldn't you be asking him why his mother, also my grandmother mind you, thought it was okay for him to you know? Ask him why he repeatedly got me pregnant and never once acknowledged it. Ask him why I've probably had more sex with him than my own husband. Ask him why we used my grandparents' house as a motel for years. Ask him why he made love to me outside his wedding reception. Hell, ask him why he married Jasmine's ass in the first place only to still come sneaking around looking for me. Yeah, Doc. He was always at my college. How many hotel bills did you have to hide from Jasmine, Mark? What about your detours to my salon when you should have been at work?"

If he thought he was going to come in here and throw me under the bus, he had another thing coming. I would tell it all. "You were always up at the salon. For what, Mark? For what? A fucking hair cut? Not every day." I now turned to look at Dr. Wardelle. "Ask him the good questions, Doc, not why do we have a difference in fuckin' opinions."

"Christian, with all due respect, we will get to that. But we need to start from where you are now, and then we will work to examine how you got here. We will get to the beginning surely. You say it's been over. Mark says it's not. You ground your answer in the fact that you haven't had sex with him for years. Is it not reasonable that we allow Mark to ground his answer?" asked Dr. Wardelle.

I was fuming. I couldn't believe Mark was lying on me, and Dr. Wardelle was going to sit there and let him. "Mark," Dr. Wardelle continued, "why do you think you and Christian have a difference of opinions about the ending of your relationship?"

This time I sat quietly, waiting to see how this nigga was about to make up some bullshit to tell my counselor.

"Christian is right. We haven't had sexual intercourse in years."

"Exactly", I said, "so what the fuck are you talking about it ain't over?"

"But," he said. Oh shit, here comes the damn but. *But what?* I thought. "But Christian and I..." he drifted off. Christian and I what? I wanted to scream. Spit it out. "Christian and I, we have sexual tension between us. We always have," he finally said.

"Tension is not sex, Mark," I yelled. "Our shit has been over for years, face it," I said, pointing my finger in his face.

"Christian, please," Dr. Wardelle interrupted.

"I knew this wasn't going to be a good idea," I said. Then I pointed to Mark. "And I can't believe you would sit here and act like we have continued a relationship. When I married Kory, that was it, and you fuckin' know it. Because you couldn't leave me alone after you married that dumb tart Jasmine, stop frontin' on me." I was too outdone. I could have slapped Mark at that moment. But he sat there just as calmly as Dr. Wardelle.

Then Mark started up again like I hadn't gone completely off on him. I could tell he was contemplating what he was about to say next. I guess I didn't get that trait from the Johnson's because I said whatever I wanted and thought about it later. Mark looked at Dr. Wardelle.

117

I knew I'd hurt his feelings, I wanted to. But he burst my bubble good when he said, "I love her. I know we haven't...you know...in quite a long time. She's right, it's been years. But it's not because we haven't wanted to. We've almost ended up in bed together many times over the years. We've done other things. Not intercourse exactly, but other things, things that we can't tell anyone about. So, I hear what she's saying," then he turned to look at me, "but I am not 100 percent sure that we won't end up in bed again, especially if we don't get help. That's really why I agreed to come here today. We've had too many close calls. We both agreed a long time ago that being found out would ruin our entire family. But we've been careless more times than I can count, and I want it to stop. I don't want our families' lives to be ruined by what we have chosen to do. Still choose to do."

I listened without saying a word because I knew he was right. We had been very careless at times, and we were almost discovered too many times to talk about. I remember after KJ passed, my friends had basically abandoned our friendship. I needed Kory and my dad to tell me that what I was feeling was okay. That it was normal for me to want to take a gun out of my house and shoot every one of those bitches for the way they treated me. They were supposed to tell me that I was not crazy at all and that all those so called ex-friends of mine were wrong...dead wrong. Even if my dad and Kory felt like that, they didn't say it. They didn't necessarily say that I was wrong, but I just didn't feel like they were on my side.

But who was there, Johnny on the spot? Uncle Mark. He said all of the right things. He understood my pain, he said. He told me that I was justified. He understood that my so-called friends had abandoned me at the worst time in my life. He understood that I wasn't crazy at all for wanting to shoot them. Hell, I wasn't trying to kill them, but I wanted them to hurt the way I was hurting, and Mark seemed to be the only one who understood that. He came over sometimes three times in one day to check on me. One afternoon, Mark and I sat in my living room in the dark for hours while he rocked me while I cried and repeatedly told me that it was going to be okay. Then we started kissing like two teenagers at a drive-in movie. I didn't even hear Kory come in the house.

A second before he flicked the light on, we hurriedly abandoned our tongue dance. But we were still locked in an embrace that would have caused my husband to go postal had it been any man outside of a relative. Mark started talking quickly about the issue with Sam and them, and Kory totally fell for it and was actually thanking Mark. He thought Mark was there to keep me from going off on them again. Ten more minutes and there was no telling what Kory would have walked in on. I still shuddered at the memory of our carelessness.

Mark's voice broke my trance, "I want to get help. I don't want to lust after my brother's daughter anymore. As crazy as it may seem, I love her husband Kory, but I am jealous of him and I am tired of it. I don't want to look at her pictures and feel any differently than when I look at my other nieces' photographs. I want to be able to go over to Chris and Kory's house for visits and be okay with her husband being home.

"I don't want to hug her and get an erection. I don't want to rub her in places that only Kory's hands should touch. I don't want to spend another night making love to my wife wishing that is was my niece instead. That's why I do not agree that what we have is over. It is still very real to me." Now he was looking at me square in the face, and there wasn't a damn thing I could say.

I felt so stupid inside. Mark was correct, and his tirade left me feeling weak and silly for insinuating that because intercourse between us had ended that this thing with us was over. Here I'd thrown this mega baby tantrum a few minutes ago. Spoke to and about my uncle in a way that I never had before when all he was saying was that our feelings were and had always been inappropriate. Looking at him, I really felt bad. I didn't say anything. This was the first time that I ever heard my uncle speak about our relationship, so I decided I better shut up and listen.

Dr. Wardelle welcomed the silence for a few moments as he jotted down notes. I guess he'd never heard anything like this before.

"Christian, while you were in the lobby, Mark admitted that he understands that he was wrong. He knows about molestation and incest and understands that he has committed both. He understands that men and women have been incarcerated for such offenses, which mean that he admits to breaking the law." I nodded. "Mark, how do you feel about Christian right now? What is it like sitting in this room next to your niece?"

Mark stalled before answering. "I'm terrified," he replied.

"Well, Mark, that's understandable considering the circumstances. I am not here to judge. I am here to explore the dynamics of your relationship with my client and how that relationship has impacted my client's life. Simple as that."

Humph, I thought to myself. Nothing with Dr. Wardelle is ever simple.

"Mark, can you tell me about your life as it is today?"

"Well, I am married. My wife is an attorney. I have four children, two who are in college studying law. One is in high school and one is in middle school. I am an audio and film producer for WXYZ. I golf and swim for recreation. I like to travel. I have never done drugs, and I drink occasionally. That's about it."

"Great, sounds like you've done all right for yourself." Dr. Wardelle smiled and nodded. He looked at Mark again and asked, "Do you remember when Christian was born?"

"I do," Mark answered quickly. "I was young, but I remember it because my mother made such a big fuss about it. I remember a lot of whispering among everyone else and then the next thing I knew, my brother brought over his new wife and their baby girl, Chris. I was about seven or eight, I guess."

"How did you feel about her being born?"

"It really wasn't a big deal to me although everyone else thought so. I am the youngest sibling in my family, so my brothers and sisters had been having children for quite some time when Chris was born. I had a gang of nieces and nephews already. Christian was the baby of the bunch for a while, so she got the most attention from us."

"Christian told me that she stayed at your house a lot while she was growing up. Was that normal? Did your other nieces and nephews stay at your house a lot, too?"

"Sometimes, but I think Christian stayed the most."

"Were you the fondest of Christian?"

Now, I was not sure about Mark, but I knew where this line of questioning was headed.

"I guess so," said Mark in sort of an uncomfortable way.

Dr. Wardelle pushed further, "Did any of your nieces or nephews sleep in the room with you when they stayed over?"

I thought Mark got it now.

"Some of my nephews did. I have three nephews that are very close to my age, so we hung out a lot together before they moved to Texas. When they visited, yes, they slept in my room." Mark was trying to be evasive I see.

But Dr. Wardelle was on it. He finally asked Mark flat out, "What about your nieces? Did they also sleep in your room?"

"No", Mark said quickly, "none of my nieces stayed in my room." I always wondered the same thing. I wondered if Mark had ever you know...with any of my cousins. So I was glad Dr. Wardelle asked him. I was also glad to know that Mark said no.

"What was it that made you want to have Christian, your niece sleep in your room with you since you never practiced this with any of your other nieces?" Dr. Wardelle asked.

Mark looked ashamed. "I don't know," he stuttered.

"When did you first think it was okay for Christian to spend time in your bedroom?"

"Umm, umm." Mark was stuttering again. "It didn't start out with Chris coming into my room. It was a long time before we went to my room," he said even though I could tell he knew that his answer wasn't what Dr. Wardelle was looking for. But Dr. Wardelle, true to form, was as smooth as ever.

"Mark, can you explain how you and Christian began to have a different relationship than you had with other relatives?" Mark couldn't get out of this one. Dr. Wardelle had backed Mark into a corner, a corner that I knew all too well. He was good for that shit. When you thought you'd wormed your way around one of his questions, he came back for the juggler. This time, though, it was on Mark.

"My brother dropped Christian off at our house a lot more than any of my other siblings. All of my other siblings were married. But Mel was raising Christian on his own. He'd tried a few sitters I think, but none of them worked, and he would drop her off a lot at our house because there was usually someone there to watch her. Since I was the baby of the bunch, I was like the built in babysitter. Melvin spoiled me. He even paid for my first car. All I had to do," his voice trailed off, "was take care of Christian."

"I understand that," said Dr. Wardelle as if he was intrigued by Mark's explanation, "but I want to know the turning point. When did you stop babysitting her and begin treating her more like a girlfriend? Was it a kiss, or a hug? What happened? Something had to happen, or we wouldn't be sitting here today discussing how to undo this 'thing' as you both refer to it.

"I can't help you do that unless I know how this thing started in the first place. I need to know what you were thinking and how those thoughts turned into actions. Does that make sense, Mr. Johnson?" Dr. Wardelle sounded like he was teaching a damn class, and Mark had some type of cognitive disability. This white man broke it all the way down for my uncle.

I assume he was starting to get Dr. Wardelle's drift and decided to come on out with it. I wish I had ear plugs because although Dr. Wardelle wanted to hear this, I most certainly did not. "Chris clung to me more than anyone else. She was so cute. All my friends adored her. She would sing and dance for them when they came over. My girlfriends treated her like a little sister; they painted her nails and stuff. My guy friends bought her ice cream off of the truck.

"I loved her. Now, don't take what I am about to say the wrong way because I am not saying that my mother didn't love Christian, I know she did, but for some reason, she was sort of mean to her at times. At first, I thought I was protecting her from my mother's wrath by taking her everywhere with me. Keeping her close to me was not so that I could ... it was really to keep her out of the line of fire with my mom."

I couldn't believe he actually admitted that the wench was mean. We had never really discussed my grandmother. It felt good to know that he realized she treated me so terribly. Mark was really paying attention back then, and although he didn't say it, he knew it was worse than that. He knew that my grandmother saw him on top of me on more than one occasion.

I could still remember how she looked at me, not her son, but me, with disgust, like I had somehow ruined her son. She used to see me on his lap all the time as well. She knew I was way too old and too developed to be sitting on my uncle's lap. They had a bathroom in the basement, and Mark and I would go down there all the time to experiment. She was putting a load of laundry in one time when we came out together and another time she was unloading groceries into the deep freezer. Did she say anything? Not at all. I couldn't even count the number of times my grandmother had an opportunity to put a stop to what she knew was going on under her very roof, and she always, always turned the other cheek to Mark and scowled at me.

"Go on," Dr. Wardelle said to Mark, ending my trip down memory lane.

"I was getting to the age when I thought about sex a lot. I used to sneak my older brother's porn magazines."

Mark stopped, but Dr. Wardelle urged him to continue.

"This is so terrible," said Mark. "I don't think I can do this. I thought I was ready for this, but maybe I'm not. Maybe I should come back at a different time."

Dr. Wardelle wasn't letting him off the hook that easily. "Mark, if this was only about you, I would let you get up and walk out of here, and it would be totally up to you if you ever called to schedule another appointment. But, I've been working with Christian on and off for several years, and I have pushed her to a place where she finally feels safe enough to reveal where her pain originates.

"Christian has told me repeatedly that her pain is related to Carmen and Carmen alone. She doesn't blame you at all for her unhappiness, but she does blame the ones who she felt should have protected her from you. So, you need to understand that your actions, past and present, play a huge role in her life. Your 'uncle turned boyfriend' type of role has totally confused Mrs. Banks.

"I know for a fact that she loves her husband, but she doesn't even protect him the way she protects you. Do you remember that Christian had Kory put in jail for assault. She actually invited scrutiny into their lives when Mr. Banks broke the law. But, you? You? You she protects to no end. Her love runs deep for you, Mr. Johnson. So you see, you really need to help her understand how this 'thing' you two have was conceived.

"If you two do not get help soon, this 'thing' you are toying with is going to blow and so many people are going to be hurt. Hasn't your family suffered enough? Haven't you suffered enough? Allow me to help you and Mrs. Banks break this tangled web of affection and begin to build a normal familial relationship. It's not too late."

I was crying now, because again, I felt sorry for Mark. I wanted to reach out and hug him or at least grab his hand, but I was too chicken to even look at him. I was used to Dr. Wardelle getting in my ass, but this was new for Mark. He was in unchartered territory. He hadn't been talked to like this before. Mark was right; he probably wasn't ready for this. Dr. Wardelle was also right; I did still love this man who was sitting next to me having a hard time opening up about why he loved me like he did. I'd never thought of how I protected him more than I did my own husband. I didn't love Mark like I loved Kory, but I didn't love him like I loved the rest of my uncles either. I really wanted Mark to stay and face this demon with me, but I would certainly understand if he couldn't. He was shaking his head. I knew he couldn't stay. He was drained. He got up; he didn't say a word. He never even looked up from the floor. He walked out of the room while Dr. Wardelle and I watched him leave. We never got to the bottom of how this thing began. Better luck next time. If there was a next time.

I'd left within minutes of Mark walking out of Dr. Wardelle's office. I was surprised when I approached my car because Mark was actually waiting for me in the parking garage. He was leaning against my car, and he was still visibly upset. He jumped when I turned the car alarm off.

"Christian, I'm sorry," he began to mumble. I shook my head to let him know that I didn't need an apology. I remember when Kory and I first started counseling; I wanted to walk, too. I'd had enough as well. This had nothing on what Kory and I were going through. I was actually surprised Mark lasted as long as he did.

"It's okay," I told him it was all kinds of weird. We had never talked about our thing, so I kept replaying a lot of what was said over in my mind. We had both been scolded all morning about our inappropriate relationship. I landed right into my uncle's embrace, and we stayed like that for what seemed like forever.

"I love you, baby girl. I don't think that man understands that. He thinks I am some old pervert who has a problem with young pretty girls. It's not like that, Christian. How can someone help who they love? How can you help who excites you? This thing began over 20 years ago, and I still have this thing for you. I didn't mean to make you sound like a liar."

I cut him off because I felt bad about that entire exchange. "I'm sorry, too," I said. "I kept telling myself that as long as we didn't have sex, anything else we did was fixable. I know that was a copout now. But it made me feel better to think it, you know? Then you said all of that stuff upstairs about still being in love with me and thinking about me when you shouldn't be. I feel the same way." I was saying all of this and crying, but I was not backing off my uncle. I actually felt safe right there, like he was the only one who understood. Well, really he was.

136

"And Jasmine, poor Jasmine," Mark said. "Christian, she has confronted me so many times over the years about me and you. I always made her think she was crazy and delusional. I even asked her what type of person makes such accusations."

Now, in a way this surprised me, but in some ways, it didn't. I always knew Jasmine wasn't fond of me, but I didn't like her, so it didn't really matter. We were cordial when necessary and fake enough to fool the rest of the family, but truth be told, there was no love lost between us.

"What kind of accusations?" I asked. I really needed to know because I couldn't have her messing everything up. My gut was telling me that she knew much more than I wanted her to. But if she had been quiet all of these years, then maybe not.

"Let's get in the car and talk. I have wanted to talk to you about Jasmine for a long time, but I didn't know how."

He walked around to my passenger seat, and I got in the driver's seat. I turned the car on, turned the radio on for background noise more than anything else. I didn't have long because I'd only blocked the morning out. I needed to be at the shop for my afternoon appointments. But I needed to hear this, and this Benzo wasn't going anywhere until Mark spilled the beans.

"Christian, Jasmine isn't stupid. She sensed your unwillingness to even get to know her way back when you were still in high school." Mark rambled on about Jasmine's constant remarks about everyone spoiling me and how he always defended me. But what really caught my attention was when he said that he loved me more than he loved his own wife and that he married her thinking it would cure the lustful feelings he had toward me.

Mark had me speechless when he told me about what Jasmine saw the night of my high school graduation party.

He was drunk and followed me around the party like a little puppy. Everywhere I went, when I turned around, he was right in my face. From that day forward, Jasmine kept asking him what kind of sick thing he had for me and if I was really Mel's daughter. He said she checked his phone records. She counted the number of times he called me. That's why he got the separate cell phone because he became so sick of combating her accusations. He said over the years Jasmine's accusations had gotten bolder because she outright asked him, how long had we been sleeping together.

Mark went on to tell me how they've had a physical altercation over her accusations and how awful he felt after hitting his wife. And that how she kept apologizing that she knew it was sick and that she couldn't have married a man who would do that but would turn around a few weeks later and accuse him of sleeping with me again.

139

Listening to Mark talk made me realize I was truly caught up in a web of mess. Counseling should have been making us better. It wasn't working the way it did for me and Kory. Actually, counseling was stirring up old feelings that were once dormant. After Mark told me that bizarre ass story about him and Jasmine and what she really knew, but only thought she knew, I wanted him more. We had never discussed this stuff. As a matter of fact, we never really discussed too much outside of family stuff. Dr. Wardelle was so right about so many things. Mark and I were in love with each other; even though we didn't have sex, it didn't mean that we were through with our thing, and most importantly, we couldn't be alone together.

Before Mark got out of the car after our first counseling session that should have helped us, we both felt the tension, and after several I'm sorry and we'll get past this, we'll be able to be better spouses, all of the good stuff that we should have said because it was the right thing to say, we were locked in an embrace that led to a peck on a cheek, that led to a peck on the lips. I don't know who opened first, but the next thing I knew we were French kissing in the front seat of my car. I was married, I was a mother, this was my uncle, and again, we'd come from counseling. But our attraction was so strong. His hands started up my shirt, mine down his pants.

Then he said, "Drive, Christian, get out of here, it's too risky." So I drove out of the parking lot while my uncle pleased me orally for the first time in a long time, and when I finally drove to a remote location, even though I knew it was wrong, all odds were against this, we both had families to lose, we moved to the back seat of the car and loved one another for the first time in over 10 years. Mark was so gentle. He told me that he loved me over and over again. He kept telling me that he always wished he were Kory. For a little while at least, nothing was wrong in the world. I had not been that aroused in years by anyone, Kory included, and we had a very healthy sex life. When it was over, it was obvious that we both felt terrible. I immediately became full of regret. I felt dirty.

"You know we can't tell Dr. Wardelle about this, Christian. He wouldn't understand." What kind of man pours his heart out in a counseling session only to commit the same act?"

"I think we're addicted," I said. "I read a book about it once. It's the only thing that makes sense. Why else would we throw caution to the wind for a few minutes of sex? Why?"

We drove back to the parking garage in complete silence, feeling so ashamed of what had transpired between us. When I dropped Mark off at his car, it was awkward. What did you do now? Did you deuce each other out, hug, kiss? What? I didn't want to look at Mark. I kept staring straight ahead, still replaying the last hour or so in my mind. This day had not turned out the way it was supposed to. Was I supposed to go home and be the loving wife to Kory? While I was deep, deep in thought, Mark came around to my side, and I let the window down. He leaned in and kissed me like it was no big deal that it was still daylight.

"I love you, baby girl. I don't know how all this counseling stuff is going to play out, but I know we need it more than ever. We're playing a dangerous game, Christian. I will always protect us," he said. Then he pointed to me and said, "I will always protect this, but don't you agree that this should be our last time?" he asked sort of out of nowhere.

I nodded because Mark wasn't fooling anyone; this was not going to be our last time. We'd re-ignited a flame that had been desperately waiting to burn. It's wrong, yeah, it's cheating; it's incest; it's all of those things. But I'd become so immune to giving a shit about stuff that it no longer mattered. I was going to continue the counseling sessions because they were helpful, and Dr. Wardelle did get the answers to many of the questions I've always had. But, like Mark said, we wouldn't tell him about this, and I was through making promises, trying to live right and all of that. I got all this bullshit going on with Carmen that I needed an outlet. If I wanted to fuck Mark, I was going to do it, and I wasn't going to feel bad about it. So I reached for his head and pulled him in closer to me, and we kissed for what seemed like an eternity. I needed to erase all thoughts of this being our last time from this man's mind. He'd be calling. Watch, he'd be calling, I thought as I put on my seat belt and drove home to be with my family.

Chapter 6

I had put this off long enough; it was high time that I paid my father a visit. As mad as he was with me, I was his only child, the one he doted on; he was the only person who had loved me unconditionally since the day I was born. He certainly couldn't stay mad at me forever, and I couldn't fathom my father moving clear across the country with our relationship as estranged as it was. Since today was Sunday and I had rarely taken clients on Sunday since opening the new shop, I was going to visit my daddy.

When I turned onto my father's street, my heart dropped; my car actually made a screeching sound as I turned into the driveway of my childhood home. Although I

145

was well aware that my father was preparing to marry Cassandra and move to Arizona within the next couple of months, I was not prepared to see the For Sale sign in the middle of the front yard. It made everything all too real. I sat in the car for a few minutes gearing up for the tongue lashing I was sure my father was prepared to give me. When I mustered up enough strength, I got out of the car, used the key I'd had since I was twelve years old, and opened the front door of the house that would soon belong to another family.

As if the For Sale sign wasn't enough, the brown cardboard boxes packed, taped, and lined against every wall in the house brought tears to my eyes. There was absolutely no furniture left on the first floor… nothing.

"Daddy," I yelled. "Da--ddy."

I waited and called my daddy again. As I went from room to room, I continued to yell for him before realizing that I was alone in the house. As I headed up the stairs to my old room, I began to hyperventilate. Although I hadn't slept in that room in over 17 years, I wasn't ready to see it packed up. I hoped my daddy hadn't disregarded my past like he'd done with the rest of the house. Hell, he was moving on, I wasn't. When I opened the door, a huge smile crept across my face. Although I was still sad and the tears were flowing freely, I was glad that he had left my room as it had always been. The walls were still purple. The green lava lamp was still perched on top of my computer desk. Even the old ass computer from Radio Shack was there. My high school yearbook was on the bookshelf just as I'd left it, and my favorite picture of Ronnie DeVoe from New Edition was still hanging on the wall.

I plopped down on the purple, blue and green polka dot comforter when I heard a knock at the front door. Who would be knocking on the door at this time of day? Didn't

Jehovah's Witnesses come out on Saturdays? It was Sunday for crying out loud. I didn't want to be bothered, so I ignored them. A few knocks later, I heard my name being called. Oh damn, it sounded like Kendra's black ass. The last person I wanted to see was my neighbor and backstabbing ex-friend Kendra. But my truck was in the driveway, so there was no hiding from her. This was a time when I wished it had been the Jehovah's Witnesses.

"Christian, Christian," Kendra continued to yell as she now peeked into the living room window. Finally I went downstairs and opened the door. I wasn't feeling it today and quickly let Kendra know it.

"Look, Kendra, I came over here to see my daddy, and he ain't here, so I am about to pack my old room up and leave. I'll tell him you stopped by." With that, I shut the door and turned to walk away, leaving the woman who had once been one of my closest friends standing alone on the porch. As soon as I started up the steps again, the doorbell rang. "Damn didn't the fat bitch hear me? I am not in the mood. Take your black ass back wherever you came from and leave me the fuck alone, please." But Kendra wouldn't give up. So I went back to the front door.

"What?" I screamed as I threw the door open. "I told you that I would tell him you stopped by."

"Christian, I know you are still upset with me," Kendra began, but I cut her off.

"Look, I don't have anything else to say about it. It's over and done with it. Why are you here? Why won't you leave me alone?" But this time Kendra didn't allow me to shut the door in her face. She sort of pushed her way into the space that used to be the living room.

"Chris, I know we were wrong. I didn't realize it at the time. I know you thought we were being selfish and insensitive, but please believe me, I didn't know that I was

149

wrong. I couldn't see it at the time. I thought I was being a good friend to you and giving you space. I didn't know. I know you hate me."

"Look, Kendra, I said I was over it, and I am, but let's get one thing straight, there was a time when I would have said, hell yeah, I hate each and every one of your fake asses, but I'm over it. Remember, I was so crazy that I needed meds and a shrink?" I asked sarcastically. "Well, my shrink told me how to dismiss y'all. So that's what the fuck I did, and that boo, is why none of y'all have heard from me in years. You're dismissed. Now please leave me alone, Kendra." I turned and walked up the stairs. "See yourself out."

I didn't even turn and look back, a move that turned out to bite me in the butt because when I plopped back down on my old bed, guess who plopped their fat ass right down across from me in the old lime green Papasan chair from

150

Pier One. Why didn't she get it? We hadn't talked in years, why was she here? I got up to look for some empty boxes. I secretly wished Kendra would be gone when I returned to the room, no such luck, so I turned on my old boom box. If she was going to stay in here, she wasn't going to talk me to death about being sorry and shit. I didn't want to hear that today. Really, I didn't want to hear it any day.

I was in a fucked up state of mind, and there was no way I was going to let Kendra fuck up my day any more with talk of her and those fake ass bitches that I once called friends and how they deserted me in the wake of my baby's passing. Thinking about it was making me start to sweat. Kendra better be lucky that I had more pressing issues because the sight of her mixed with thoughts of my late son could only result in one thing, an ass whooping with Kendra's name all over it. But I'd changed, so I hummed along to Rihanna. She was such a cute little thing. She was singing something about taking a bow. I didn't know why, but I liked this little song, so I was going to sing it right along with her. "You put on quite a show, really had me going, now it's time to go…"

I sang along to about six more songs as I packed up my old room, and before I knew it, Kendra was packing like she worked for Two Men, a Fat Ass, and a God Damn Truck. She had found some newspaper and everything. She was wrapping shit up, placing it all neat in the boxes. But I couldn't appreciate it because I wanted her gone.

Now I love, my Detroit radio station, I do, but they sometimes fuck it up, and today was one of those days. They'd been jamming since I turned the radio on, and here they went with the Silky Silky Soul Singer. Oh no, not on my damn boom box. So I went over and turned it down. Kendra took it as her sign to start talking. She knew how much I hated Silky Silky.

"Christian," I heard my name being called from downstairs. "Chris, you here?" I scrambled from my bed, where I was sitting listening to Kendra ramble on about her cheating husband.

"Hey baby," my daddy greeted me with a kiss on my cheek. "How you doing?" He turned toward Kendra, who was now standing right behind me.

"Hey Kendra," he greeted, smiling.

Kendra smiled back at him, "How's it going, Mr. Johnson?" she replied while walking toward the front door.

"Not bad I suppose," he replied.

"I'm really going to miss you when you move."

"I'm going to miss you, too," he replied. "We've had a lot of memories in this house." He gave Kendra a hug as she walked out the front door.

I glared at him as he closed the door. "What do you mean 'not bad, I suppose'?" I jokingly asked. We always had the perfect father-daughter relationship; we talked about mostly everything and always spent time together. But because of all the stuff that's happened in the last couple of months, we still hadn't really mended our relationship that completely fell apart when I brought Carmen to Detroit. I felt as if he had practically abandoned me when Carmen came to town, then he started dating Cassandra and that drove us farther apart.

Daddy stared at me for a moment thoughtfully. Some feelings were still rather strange to me, such as...did he still love me the same and would we ever have the same bond we once shared.

The two of us just stood there, a bit awkwardly. I was basically looking everywhere except at him. In fact, I had found a rather questionable stain on the carpet. It didn't help that my father's eyes were boring into my head. I looked up and his eyes, filled with some kind of emotion, continued to bore into my face. I found myself inching closer and closer toward him and then I finally reached out and gave him the biggest hug.

After hearing him persecute me time and time again for contacting Carmen against everyone's will, I was now beginning to understand that I'd caused the people who loved me most an insurmountable amount of pain with bringing Carmen here, a woman who I'd come to barely stand being around. It was time for me to make this right and sincerely apologize to my father.

"Daddy, we need to talk. I can't take back what is in the past, but we need to move on and mend our relationship." I made my way over to the stairs to sit down, and Daddy followed suit. "You were right about Carmen. I don't think she truly cares about me." He was quiet, he didn't even turn to look at me, and I didn't want to look at him either. "I cannot tell you how sorry I am, but I am and I

155

love you. I honestly thought that we'd get over this once things began to get back to normal. I took our relationship for granted. I was doing what I did out of love and I-" my words were quickly interrupted.

"This was out of your own selfishness, Chris, not love." His words rang through my ears. Tears began to fill my eyes. I knew my dad was hurt because his temper quickly rose; he couldn't keep the anger out of his voice, and I realized painfully, how quickly his mood changed from cheery to icy cold.

"Hmph," I replied. He was right; I was being selfish, but like he didn't get it back then, he didn't get it now; I did this because I need to know why Carmen left me.

"Chris, the situation with me and Carmen should have never been. Yes, we brought a child into this world. With everything that was going on at the time, I was able to provide a better life for you than she could when she decided to leave."

I shook my head. "What do you mean everything that was going on at the time?"

"Carmen was a junkie. She was addicted to prescription drugs. Chris, she had a lot of personal issues she was dealing with that I didn't find out until after we were married."

Through my tears, I replied, "Wow! I always thought Carmen left because you continued a relationship with Delores."

I was lost in thought for the moment, but I could hear my daddy talking, "Chris, we've talked about this. You've known for a while that I married Carmen because she was pregnant. That was supposed to be the start of our life together, but it wasn't, she was a nice woman, educated, and beautiful, but we just weren't right for each other."

157

Thinking about those words made me choke up. I just stared ahead into the air. I had never felt more horrible. I think I was trembling. I didn't even try to hold my tears back. I was so tired of faking my feelings.

We sat in silence after he said all that. Our private moment was suddenly interrupted by the sound of my cell phone ringing. I looked at the Caller ID and it read Kory.

"So you finally decided to call me back huh?" I said after picking up sounding somewhat upset.

"I was busy" Kory replied.

"Probably with some bitch," I slid in.

"Man, go somewhere with that foolishness. I was handling business." His tone indicated he didn't want an argument. "I'm calling 'cause you need to make your way home. The twins keep asking where you at."

I took in a deep breath. "And I wonder where you be at," I sarcastically replied. "Are they all right?" I asked, concerned.

"Yeah, they all right, I'm just tired of them always asking where you at."

There was a moment of silence. "I'm on my way," I replied before ending the call.

I dropped my cell phone into my purse and stood. "I have to get home to the kids, but we will sit down and talk real soon. By the way, I want to have something special for you and Cassandra to celebrate your upcoming nuptials." I smiled, while stretching to crack my bones back into place after sitting on those stairs so long.

"Okay. We would love that, Chris, thank you." A smile finally appeared on his face.

I grinned at him. "Well, it's not every day my daddy gets married and..." I paused, letting the anticipation build.

"At first, I must admit, I was worried that Cassandra wasn't going to be around long. You know how you live, love 'em and leave 'em. Right?" We both laughed. "But from what the kids and Kory have told me and the few times I have been around her, Cassandra seem to be a very nice lady."

It was about another 20 minutes before I reached the front door. Daddy's words made me believe that he was truly happy; he told me what was going on with the wedding, them moving, his plans if the house didn't sell right away, and the craziness my aunts and uncles were up to including Mark.

"Give me a hug. I love you, Chris," he said, wrapping his arms around me, holding tight.

"I love you, too, Daddy," I said before walking out the door and heading home to deal with Kory, the kids, and Carmen. As I drove home, lost in my thoughts, everything began to sink in. I'd been through the good and bad of life.

My life had been far from perfect, and I'd been suffering the consequences for my actions every day. I realized that I didn't embrace my emotions until I was going through struggle, and right now, I was confused, nervous and worried. My world felt like it was turning upside down and was crashing down on me. When I arrived home, I stepped out of my car, and my knees buckled as I made my way inside the madness of the Banks' household.

CHAPTER 7

I woke up abruptly in the morning with a knot in my stomach, my hands were shaking, and I was sweating like I had run a mile. I usually felt this way on the days I had my sessions with Dr. Wardelle, but I was extremely nervous because today was another session that included Mark. I rolled over and noticed that Kory was not in the bed; I heard him behind our closed bedroom door, fussing at Kamryn about something. All I could hear was her whining and Kory telling her he didn't want to hear whatever it was she was whining about and to go in her room and put on her shoes. Sighing, I got out of bed and headed to the bathroom. I washed my face, brushed my teeth, then I stepped out of the bathroom and opened up our bedroom door. I ran into Kory in the hallway. I laughed as I watched him running out the bathroom, chasing behind Klarke with one of her shoes in his hand.

"Baby, come here so Mommy can put on your shoe," I said, stopping Klarke dead in her tracks. After I put on Klarke's shoe, I turned and walked back into our bedroom with Kory following right behind me.

"Are you coming to the shop today?" Kory asked. I heard the hurt and pain in his voice.

"Of course, but I have a ten o'clock with Dr. Wardelle, then I will be there for my twelve o'clock client." I knew Kory was mad with me, I knew he felt neglected, but Dr. Wardelle said I was showing signs of improvement, so when I got the answers I was looking for, whatever they might be, hopefully this would bring balance into our household. Why couldn't Kory understand that he would be the one who benefited the most from my change, not Carmen or Mark?

I could tell by the way Kory was looking at me that he wanted to say something else. "What's up, babe?" I asked as Kory's eyes locked on mine.

"Chris, do you want to be here anymore? You have ignored everyone in this house. Kamryn and the twins deserve more, you're their mother. Carmen's been here for five months, and you barely pay her any attention. The only time you did pay attention to her was when she told you she wanted to go back to California. You talked her out of leaving that time because you were scared that if she left Detroit, she wouldn't come back. And the way you've been treating her, I wouldn't blame her if she left and didn't come back. And what about me? Do you still love me?"

"I can't believe you have to ask me that. Of course I love you," I replied as I moved Kory out the way so I could get dressed for my ten o'clock appointment with Dr. Wardelle. As I looked through my closet, I thought about what Kory asked me, and I concluded him asking his question was to cover up for his own infidelity.

Kory took a deep breath and shook his head. As he walked out the bedroom, as if he was trying hard not to start another argument, he said, "I'm out. I'll see you at the shop." Dealing with my situation in regards to Carmen and Mark was far more personal to me than anything else I had ever experienced in life, and I had no one to talk to about this but Dr. Wardelle.

As I drove in the direction toward Dr. Wardelle's office for the second session that included Mark, my heart began beating fast. Mark originally agreed to six counseling sessions. After the way the first session ended, I wasn't sure that he would return.

When I arrived at Dr. Wardelle's office, Mark was already waiting in the lobby. Looking at Mark made me realize I wasn't ready for today's session. After Dr. Wardelle greeted us both with a hello, he wasted no time picking up exactly where the last session left off.

My eyes twitched rapidly back and forth between the two individuals that sat before me. I started to ache from head to toe; I swear I actually felt my heart crack open. I rubbed my eyes, feeling the imaginary headache as Mark began to speak.

"Like I said, I used to look at my brothers' porn magazines, and I would start to feel some kind of way. I experienced my first erection that I can remember while looking at those magazines. It got so bad that I would sneak in their rooms whenever I could to look at the pictures and get off. But then they moved out. They took their magazines with them I guess. I knew they were no longer there. I liked the feeling I had when I looked at them, but didn't really realize I missed the feeling until one day when Christian was over and sat on my lap. I knew she wasn't doing it on purpose, but she kept moving around. Her squirming quickly gave me that feeling again.

"The same feeling you got from looking at the pornographic magazines, you also got from your niece. Is that correct?" Dr. Wardelle asked.

Mark nodded. "Before I knew it, I had an erection. Of course she didn't know what it was, and she continued to move around all over my lap. I knew I should have moved her off of me, but I didn't. I liked the feeling way too much. I let her move around on my lap until I... you know. I ejaculated."

Oh my God! I felt horrible. I was the one who started this. I jumped my happy ass right on top of his lap and wiggled my young tail around so much that my uncle, who was completely innocent at the time, came right there in his young teenaged Levis. Oh my God. I felt awful.

"Mark, what happened that day right after you ejaculated?"

"I sat there for a few minutes. I couldn't believe what had happened, and I knew I couldn't tell anyone about it. I mean I would have told my boys, but it wasn't some girl from school, it was my younger niece that they all knew and loved. I loved her, too. I felt awful and perverted. I swear I did. I finally told her that I had to go to the bathroom, and I went to wash up. I said to myself, that I was never allowing her to sit on my lap again. Ever."

"What happened then, Mark? How did Christian get back on your lap?"

"Like I said, she was always over. After that first time, I kept her off of my lap and away from me for about a month. Then one day she was over, I was ignoring her, and my dad said that she was in the backyard crying. I asked her what was wrong although I kind of knew already because I kept telling her to go outside and play. I kept pushing her, not physically, away.

"She said that I didn't want to play with her anymore. She asked me why I didn't love her anymore. I felt bad. I didn't want her to be sad. I never wanted her to be sad. Plus, I thought that since so much time had passed that it might be okay to let her hang out with me again. But when she ran and jumped on me, I got an instant erection. I actually dropped her because I was in shock that it had happened again."

"I remember that," I said. "I didn't know why you dropped me. You said something about me being heavy, didn't you? I had no idea."

"I said something like that, I don't know, but to make matters worse, she started crying. I didn't want my parents to come out back, see her crying and me with an erection, so I scooped her up again."

"I started telling you that my body hurt," I said.

"Exactly, and I started rubbing you. In my mind, I told myself I was rubbing you to make you feel better, but really, I rubbed you to make myself feel better. From that day on, every time she was around, I was aroused. I told myself that since she didn't know what it was, I wasn't doing anything wrong. I said that I wouldn't rub her anymore because that would be wrong, but I didn't stop her from sitting on my lap, and she always sat on my lap."

"If you say that you weren't going to touch her, how did it progress beyond touching?" said Dr. Wardelle.

"Well, the lap thing lasted for a long time. Nothing else, the lap thing. Occasionally, she'd hug me if she was leaving to go with her dad or something, but mostly it was the lap thing. Then, one day she came over directly from

170

dance class. She was still dressed in her dance outfit or whatever. I saw her and left out the house immediately. I knew she couldn't sit on my lap, not that day, not with that on. But my father was also leaving, and my mother wasn't home, so he called me back in the house and told me to either take her with me or stay there with her until my brother came to pick her up. As soon as I sat down, she hopped on my lap all excited to tell me about her dance class. She started trying to show me the moves, but she stayed on my lap. I kept telling her to stand on the floor and show me, but she wouldn't move.

"I thought to myself that she liked being on my lap as much as I enjoyed it. There had to be a reason why she would gyrate on my lap when I clearly kept asking her to get up. Plus she was getting a little older, too, really too old to be sitting on anyone's lap."

"Did you use these things, Christian was getting older, but still sat on your lap or Christian gyrated while on your lap even when you asked to get up… did you use those things, Mark, to ease your conscience?" Dr. Wardelle asked.

"I rationalized in my mind that she liked it. So I stopped fighting my urges. In the past, I had only allowed her to move around on my lap, which aroused me, but that day was the first time I put my hands around her hips and actually bounced her up and down on top of me. When I heard her moan, I ejaculated like never before."

He was sweating now. This had to be rough for him. It's crazy how he remembered it so vividly because I did, too. I remembered every single time that I crawled directly into the line of fire.

Mark continued. I guess he felt like he wanted it all out, and honestly I couldn't blame him. "I knew I had crossed the line. I should have stopped right then, but I always wanted that initial feeling that I got from looking at those porn mags. I told myself that if she liked it, it wasn't wrong."

Now Dr. Wardelle was looking at me, and the sweat beads began to form around my nose. I really hoped my deodorant was working because I knew all too well how Dr. Wardelle could be. "Christian, as you sit here and listen to your uncle's recollection of how this relationship with you two progressed, how does it make you feel? Are there things that don't seem right to you? Do you remember it the same way that Mark remembers it?"

"Yes, it's the way I remember it," I said cowardly. I did not want to talk about how it made me feel to hear Mark divulge such an intimate and personal part of our lives that only he knew. No, I really didn't want to talk about my feelings. But Dr. Wardelle would never let anyone off of the hook that easily, so again he asked me, "Christian, how does it make you feel to listen to Mark describe the birth of your relationship? Turn to Mark and tell him how hearing what he said made you feel."

I turned and looked at Mark. He couldn't look at me though. I was thinking, now Dr. Wardelle, you told me to look at him, but you aren't telling him to look at me. Then I realized I was being petty, so I started talking. It was actually easier to talk without him looking at me anyway.

"Hearing you talk about this is hard for me. I've always blamed myself for what happened between us and hearing you describe how things happened didn't negate that. I still feel totally responsible. I can hear your voice telling me over and over again to either be still or get down. But I never did. I don't ever remember removing myself from your lap." I got quiet and shook my head. This was worse than I imagined. I wanted Mark to be a horny teenaged boy who forced himself on me and that was that.

Even though I knew in my heart that wasn't true, I wanted it to be. It would have exonerated my role in this madness.

"Christian," Dr. Wardelle said. "This isn't about blame. Humans often misplace blame so that they can free themselves from the guilt. But, I must say, both you and Mark have seemed to accept responsibility for your actions, so there is no need for blame."

I nodded, but I still felt totally guilty.

"Mark, how long did this type of behavior go on before it progressed to full sexual intercourse?" asked Dr. Wardelle.

"Not long because it was like a drug. I kept chasing that first feeling, and each time she was over, I needed more than what we'd done before. I always thought that if she ever chose not to sit on my lap then that would be a sign that she didn't want to be a part of our lap thing anymore, and I'd stop. But she always sat on my lap."

My head was hung really low then. Because Mark was right. It only took me a few times to sit on his lap to realize that there was something different about sitting on Mark's lap than any other lap I'd ever sat on. He's also right that I could have chosen to sit next to him on the couch or in another chair, but I didn't. There was something about the contact that I liked, too.

Mark was still talking, and it snapped me out of my thought. "Then she sat on my lap one day when I had boxer shorts on." I sensed the uneasiness in Mark's voice. Then he stopped talking altogether. I witnessed my uncle cry like a baby. I hadn't seen him cry this hard since my grandmother died. I thought I'd cried so much about this that my tears were non-existent. But I knew why he was crying. Dr. Wardelle was taking to him a place he hadn't visited in years. Dr. Wardelle was going to make Mark face his own demons one by one. Mark was already beginning to admit that he used my body for his sexual pleasure, but Dr. Wardelle wanted more. He wanted to know it all.

"So you had boxer shorts on, no other pants, shorts, jeans, nothing like that?" Dr. Wardelle asked.

"Just the boxers," said Mark.

"And Christian, was about how old?"

"She was about 13 or 14, I would guess." I nodded in agreement, and Mark continued. "We were watching TV like we always did when she came over. Music videos were our thing. I actually had a cover over me lying on the couch. She came and climbed under the cover and at first laid with me on the couch. We were actually at opposite ends. I thought, great, nothing can happen now. But two of us lying on the couch, soon became cramped, so I sat up and allowed her to continue lying down. But as soon as I sat up, so did she. Within about two minutes, she was on my lap and of course, I welcomed it."

Mark was shaking his head as if he couldn't even believe what he was saying. "As soon as she sat on my lap, she started moving around, dancing to the videos. She had on the shortest of shorts, and all I know is..." he stopped. Mark was frozen. Dr. Wardelle looked at Mark encouragingly and nodded. I was staring straight at Dr. Wardelle who was staring at Mark who was counting the tiles on Dr. Wardelle's office floor. "I became aroused. Parts of my body could no longer be contained by my boxer shorts. I should have gotten up."

He shook his head. "Because I knew what I wanted to do. But I was so scared. Up until this time, I didn't think Christian knew what was going on. So I was scared that if I took it any further, that she would freak and tell my brother. So I sat as still as I could. But it didn't matter because she was moving all over the place. I cowardly leaned back on the couch and let my niece..." His voice trailed off again.

"Let your niece do what?" Dr. Wardelle pressed. Mark didn't answer. He sat there looking at the floor, shaking his head. But his lips were glued shut. Somehow his courage to say the things he'd revealed gave me a little courage, so I stepped in.

"He let his niece ride him," I said matter of fact like. But then I started crying. I cried so hard I didn't even know if they understood me as I confessed, "He's right. I had on shorts that I'd cut extra short because that's what me and all my friends did. He's right, he was lying down and there were several places that I could have gone, but I purposely laid right up under him and secretly wished for him to sit up. Oh God, I can't believe I'm saying this, but I wanted to sit on his lap.

"I looked forward to sitting on his lap. I didn't know what it did to him. I didn't know about this *feeling* he's talking about. But I knew it made him feel good. I could see

179

it in his face. I liked making him feel good. I thought if I made him feel good, he'd always be around or better yet, he'd always want me around. So when he sat up that day to allow me to lie more comfortably, I jumped my fast ass right on top of him.

"I felt his penis stiffening right away. That made me feel powerful. I had an effect on Mark that I thought no one else did. I was happy about that. So I moved around harder and gyrated deeper, I wanted to see how hard I could get him.

"Then my shorts and underwear began to shift due to the gyrating. Not because of Mark, but because of Christian. And when he leaned back against the couch, I realized that more of his penis was uncovered and I purposely moved myself around so that he could enter me, and that was the first time we had intercourse. That was the beginning of this thing we had. That was the day I fell in love with my uncle.

180

From that day on, I would have done any fuckin' thing to make Mark happy."

Although I was still sobbing uncontrollably, I was on a roll. I had wanted to say this for so long. I needed Mark to hear how I felt. I didn't want him to beat himself up about something that I so desperately wanted. I wanted him to know that I didn't blame him. Even if I should, I didn't. Both Mark and Dr. Wardelle were speechless, so I kept speaking.

"There were times when I knew Mark was trying to leave the house because he saw me coming. But I still managed to throw myself at him in some sort of way. Mark would have girls at the house that I knew he was dating, but as soon as he would get up to go to the bathroom or the kitchen, it didn't matter, I would be there waiting. You know how I learned about oral sex? Huh? Huh?" I said, getting louder.

"I learned how to provide oral sex because I was waiting for Mark in the bathroom one time when he had a girl over. He flat out told me no as soon as he walked in. I think he tried to push me out of the bathroom, but I wouldn't go. He had to use the bathroom, so he pulled out his penis ignoring the fact that I hadn't left. He wanted to get back to the pretty, high school senior waiting in my grandparents' living room on the couch where I gave my virginity away, and it made me feel so useless.

"I thought that she must be making Mark ejaculate, so he didn't need me anymore. So before he could grab his pants and pull them up, I ...I did the only thing I thought I could do. Mark liked it. I could tell by the look on his face. In my mind, I'd won. It didn't even matter if he went back and entertained his company. I felt like he still needed me. I needed to feel needed by Mark. There was no way I was going to let him abandon me. I would have done anything!" I was on the verge of hyperventilating.

I loved him. I would have done anything to continue this thing we had. It's this thing that kept me in an emotional prison. It's this thing that allowed me to fantasize about being with Mark for real even though I knew it couldn't be. It's this thing that allowed me to hate my grandmother for making me have an abortion. It's this thing that made me lie to girls about Mark so they wouldn't like him. It's this thing that had me fucking my uncle more than my boyfriend in college. It's this thing that forbade us to be alone with each other.

"You were right, Dr. Wardelle. I have felt like that for years." Although I didn't respect Mark's marriage, he tried to respect mine and even though he'd flirt, he'd never pushed. He'd backed off. I didn't want that. I didn't want him to back off. I liked when he cornered me at family dinners and pushed up on me. I liked when he copped free feels when he thought no one was looking. I liked that at every family picnic we'd attended over the last ten years, he'd offer to accompany me back to the store when I conveniently said I forgot something.

I was married, very married, and I would sit in that driver's seat and let him have his way with me, but he wouldn't initiate intercourse anymore and although that should have made me happy, it didn't. I soooo wanted him to.

I knew this was some sick shit. I knew it was. But even after that first counseling session when Mark and I ended up in the parking lot, and he got in my car, I got stiff because I knew that with one wrong move, I would have allowed Mark to love me any way he wanted in plain view of anyone walking in that garage. See, something was wrong with me; this 'thing' had totally clouded my view of

184

reality so badly that it made me want to bear a child for Mark. And I don't know, maybe I did.

CHAPTER 8

My evening client wasn't due to arrive at the shop for another two hours, so I decided to take a break and come home for lunch and possibly take a quick nap. When I arrived home, Kory's truck was parked in the driveway; he left the shop an hour earlier stating he had a few errands to run.

After I unlocked the back door and pushed it opened, my eyes were instantly drawn to four duffle bags belonging to Carmen neatly sitting in a row by the kitchen table. I could hear the television blaring on full volume from inside the sitting room. I walked toward the sitting room and there was Carmen sitting on the couch, drinking a beer, smoking a cigarette, and watching *One Life to Live*. If looks could kill Carmen would be flatlined. I stood in the walkway staring at Carmen who had now directed her attention from the television and was now looking at me.

"You're leaving me again!?" I screamed as I stood in the large open space that separated our sitting room and the hallway.

Carmen sighed sadly. "I know that you might be upset, but..."

"You're really leaving me again?" I accused, cutting Carmen off mid-sentence. "Why? So you can be alone and drink all day? Or is it so you can be with Kameko since it seems like she's the only child you claim?" I eyed the beer in her hand; tears began falling from my eyes as I clenched my fist.

A few seconds later, Kory came jogging down the stairs. He stopped dead in his tracks when he saw me standing in the hallway with my hand on my hip. "Don't

even go there, Chris," Kory interrupted; I cut an eye at him.

"You're supposed to be on my side," I yelled at him.

"So you're leaving me again?" I turned and was now facing

Carmen; my brain was still processing what was happening,

so I repeated my question because I was pretty sure Carmen

still hadn't answered my question. "You're not going to say

anything?"

"Yes, Christian, I'm leaving, but..."

I interrupted her once again. "What do you mean *yes

Christian I'm leaving but?*" It was true, I was losing Carmen

again. My head was spinning and began to throb.

I took a deep breath and angrily stared at Kory. "How

could you?" I snapped.

"How could I what?" he asked.

I looked away from Kory. A tear slipped down my

cheek; I felt betrayed. I wiped it away furiously. "How

long?" I persisted. "How long have you known she was leaving?"

"About two months," he admitted as he watched the tears roll from my eyes.

I nodded, biting my bottom lip, trying to keep myself from beating him senseless. I shook my head and began to pace in the hallway outside of the sitting room. "Two months, that's real fucked up, Kory, real fucked up. I can't deal with this shit right now, I can't." I stepped back into the room to continue my conversation with Carmen. "This is real fucked up, Carmen. So you were going to up and leave and not say goodbye. Fuck me, huh! After all that I put into mending this relationship, you're going to give up on me again and move back to L.A.?"

"Christian, please calm down," Carmen said as if she was trying to comfort me.

189

"Don't tell me to calm down." I threw my hands in the air. "How dare you tell me to calm down! How! How do you expect me to calm down?"

"Are you done making a fool out of yourself?" Kory asked.

"What!?"

"Christian, if you calm down and let me talk instead of yelling, then I can explain," Carmen said. "I'm only moving out on my own. I was approved for an apartment here in Detroit. I'm not moving back to L.A., not now anyway."

Idiot, idiot, idiot, what have I done? I thought as I listened to Carmen speak. "Why didn't y'all say that in the beginning?" I asked, embarrassed.

"Maybe next time you'll keep your mouth shut and listen," Kory shouted angrily.

I glanced over in the direction where he was standing. "I'll deal with you in a minute. That's great, Carmen. I'm glad you're moving out on your own, but why am I now hearing about this?"

"It all happened so fast, a few weeks ago Kory took me downtown to sign up for housing assistance, and then he called one of his friends, and they had my name moved up the list. The housing people called me last week, saying I was approved for an apartment and that I could move in immediately. Kory bought me furniture and it was delivered yesterday. Christian, I really wanted to surprise you."

Okay, maybe I was hearing things. Did she say Kory knew all about this, and he didn't mention anything to me about it? "Yeah, Kory is real good with keeping secrets." I cocked my head to the side, eyeing Kory with amazement.

"Are you serious? Christian, you're the one who runs in and out of this house like you're the only one who lives here. You do have a family that includes a husband and three kids, and by your actions, it seems like you don't give a damn. It's all about Christian." Kory's voice echoed throughout the room.

"All about me? Kory, stop it, you're the one who is never at home. Are you cheating?"

"That's the second time in the past month that you've made a slick ass comment about me cheating. We've been through too much for you not to trust me."

I could tell by Kory's serious facial expression that I had hit a chord. "Oh, don't act like you're not capable of cheating."

"Get the fuck out of here. If you're going to accuse me of something, get your facts straight or try focusing on your home life a little more."

"Hell yeah, I'm accusing you. When I call you, you rush me off the phone because you're walking into a meeting here, meeting this person there or its The Hundred Black Men need you to speak at this event." I said trying to cover up my guilt with accusations of him cheating and I wasn't backing down.

"I'm out in the streets everyday handling business. How do you think you're able to keep money in your pockets?" he sarcastically questioned as I walked away toward the kitchen.

Kory walked up behind me as I was getting a drink of water.

"I'm sorry," he said, placing his hands on my waist. "I really am."

I didn't care; all I knew was that he had betrayed my trust. I was tempted to move away, but figured that it wouldn't really help anything. Instead, I turned away from the sink and faced him. If I wasn't so mad at him, I might actually think he looked sexy with his guilty eyes and his hands on my hips. No, I was angry at him.

Clearing my throat, I looked into his eyes, chuckled, and pushed him slightly. "Smart ass." I might be able to ditch a boyfriend, but Kory was a lot more than that to me; he was my husband, so whatever we were going through, we were going to have to work through it.

The argument Kory and I finished having was emotionally demanding, leaving me feeling drained. I couldn't talk to them right now, my head was spinning, and I couldn't think straight. As Kory was walking out the door, I decided to ride with him and Carmen to her new apartment. I wanted to show them both that I was sorry because it was verbally hard for me to say.

When we arrived at the apartment, random furniture and boxes were still scattered around the living room, leftover from the delivery drivers. Carmen began walking around the room settling into her new apartment, the one she loved on sight. The building was old, but I did like the small terrace with the nice view of the city and the modern kitchen with the sleek design hardwood floors. The walls were painted a soothing, warm, buttery yellow which matched perfect with the dark brown leather sofa and matching chair. There was a sharp contrast between the contemporary furniture and classical form and structure of the apartment.

"We have to go shopping for décor," I said, smiling at Carmen. I've always loved decorating.

"Yes, that would be nice, Chris, but I don't need much more," Carmen replied.

Kory brought in a few of Carmen's bags along with the new CD player he purchased for her. As Carmen unpacked her bags, her rich melodic voice filled the apartment singing along to her favorite song "So Amazing" by Luther Vandross.

I stood up from the couch, grabbed my purse, and walked to the door, "Call if you need anything, all right?" I offered as Kory and I walked out the door. Even though I knew Carmen having her own place was probably best for both of us, I still didn't like the way I felt knowing that she was gone from our home.

CHAPTER 9

I had a wedding party to do, so that meant I would be at the shop early. I hated wedding parties; they got on my last nerves. There were always fifteen heffas all wanting to look different from the other, though requesting the same hair style. But this was Melissa's wedding, and me and Melissa went way back. She started coming to me when I was in hair school and had followed me everywhere even when I was temporarily doing hair in my basement. Melissa was faithful to me, so for her, I would endure these divas coming in here getting on my goddamn nerves. I knew most of the bridesmaids anyway. Melissa asked me to be in the wedding, but there was no way I could be in the wedding and do all of their hair. Even the flower girls were being brought to the shop.

It was clear that I probably wouldn't make it to the ceremony, I almost never did, but I would make it my business to get out of here in time for the reception. When I got to the shop, they were all prepped, and my assistants had put them under the dryers. I was ecstatic. I went back into my office to eat my breakfast when Mark called. He told me he was outside and that he had something to show me. I went out to the back, but guess who had already beat me out there? My sister-in- law Marcella Japs' hot ass.

I heard her squealing from a mile away. I had to admit, his new truck, the Mercedes-Benz G-Class G550 Sport Utility truck that all of us had been looking at for months now was hot! Mark told Marcella and me that he'd purchased two, one for him and one for Jasmine. I knew it shouldn't have mattered, but my heart sank. I knew Mark was my uncle, I knew he was married and that it was perfectly acceptable for him to buy his wife any vehicle that he wanted to, even if it was a one hundred and twenty thousand dollar vehicle, but it still stung. No matter what Mark said as far as his feelings for her, I believed that Mark did love Jasmine and that hurt me even if it shouldn't have.

"Mark, this is the exact truck that Lance and I were looking at the other day. Lance wasn't sold on it, but I love it!" Marcella continued to squeal. "I love it." She jumped in the passenger side and put on her sunglasses. This heffa was taking pictures of herself with her phone undoubtedly uploading them to Facebook or Instagram. I couldn't help but laugh at her.

Even though I was laughing, Mark knew better. "What's wrong, baby girl?" he asked. "Don't tell me it's nothing because I know you, remember?" I stood against the rear of his truck, shaking my head. "Are you upset because I bought Jasmine this truck, Christian?" he whispered. Marcella wouldn't have heard his ass anyway; she had turned up the radio and was singing about putting a ring on it; she was in her element.

"It's cool, Mark. She's your wife. Of course you can buy her a car. I mean Kory has bought all but one of the cars I've ever had and that's only because my dad bought me one when I turned sixteen. So of course, you can buy your wife a car." I emphasized "wife."

"Don't do me like that, Christian. You are right, she is my wife and no matter what our marriage has become, I still have obligations."

"You don't owe me any explanations, Mark. I'm your niece, she's your wife. I like the truck, but clearly not as much as Marcella," I said, sort of laughing.

This bitch was too much; she got out of the car, one stiletto at a time. Now Marcella was as cute as she wanted to be, so looking like a supermodel on the red carpet wasn't new to her, but I had never seen her step so glamorously out of a damn car. We stood there and watched the show as she sashayed her ass around that damn truck putting JLo's grand entrances to shame. She looked at us like we were the damn paparazzi. Without saying a word, Mark hit a button which started the ignition and opened the door for your majesty. She stepped in the driver's side of the truck as elegantly as she'd gotten out of the passenger's side. Then next thing I knew, Marcella Japs had taken off in the truck, and we were left looking at the temporary tag peel out of the parking lot.

"You okay," Mark said, looking me straight into my eyes. I hated when he did that. Don't look me in my eyes. I hate that. Well I really loved it, but I couldn't take it, not here, not today.

"I'm fine, Unc," I said.

"Have you talked to your dad?"

"Yeah, I went over there, but we didn't get to fully resolve anything because I had to leave....family issues."

"Chris, can you believe your pops is leaving soon? That Cassandra woman has him open. He is totally in love with her. I have never seen him like this with any woman, and my brother has had his fair share of women. Go see him again, baby girl. Your pops needs you. He's getting ready to make a major move. He needs your support even if he doesn't say it."

Your majesty whipped back in front of us, smiling like she'd hit the jackpot. "Hey good looking," she yelled out at Mark.

"What's up, beautiful?" he replied. What was this man trying to do to me? First he flaunted the fact that he'd bought Jasmine a car and now here he was making small talk with my best friend and calling her ass beautiful. Now, she was a beauty, ain't gone lie, but damn, Mark.

Marcella put the truck in park and hopped out. "Mark, I love this truck. It rides so smooth," she said. I didn't like the way her ass was saying *rides*. There was something sexual about her statement. I had known Marcella too long. "Sure wish I was Jasmine and that I had one of these bad boys."

"If you play your cards right," he replied and then they burst out laughing, but I didn't find anything funny.

"Your better stop playing with me, Mister," Marcella said. "Shit, my marriage ain't as strong as yours is." She laughed it off, but she was dead serious.

As I walked away from Marcella and Mark, I leaned into Marcella's ear and whispered, "He's married, whore."

Do you know this bitch replied, "So am I!" Oooh, she was fucking with me. The entire time I worked on Melissa's wedding party's hair, I thought about Marcella and Mark. What were they in back of the building talking about? I knew Marcella would bed Mark at the drop of a dime. She was still unhappy in her marriage. I had always known that she had a secret crush on Mark. The question was, would Mark bite? Would he really start creeping around with my best friend? Could I really handle that? Would I still be able to be cool with Marcella? Maybe that was what needed to happen. That would stop this thing between me and Mark directly in its tracks. There was no way I would still be attracted to him the way that I was if he was messing with Marcella. Me and Marcella shared a lot, but a man? Naw, I wouldn't be able to do that. So I zoned out while doing bridal style after style and thought back to me and Marcella's dinner a few days ago.

As Marcella and I ordered round after round of Lemon Drop shots, I sat there wishing that I could open up to Marcella about Mark. Talking to Dr. Wardelle was fine, but I needed to talk to my girl, you know? There was nothing like your crew. I started humming, *luvin my crew.* However, for several reasons, including the fact that I was married to her brother, I had to shake this girlfriendish moment off and get myself back together. During the dinner, I kept drifting off into deep thought. I heard Marcella calling my name while waving her hand in front of my face. Dammit, she beat me to it. She actually brought up Mark. I swear this girl could read minds.

Marcella went on to tell me how she'd seen Mark not too long ago when he'd come into Japs and they had a few drinks together while shooting the shit. I was feeling some kind of way as she was telling me this. I really couldn't say anything. I felt like I was in my 20's. I wanted to get out my phone and start texting his ass. I wanted to say, "So you fucking Marcella now? What does she have that I don't?" But I wasn't in my 20's, and this wasn't Kory we were talking about, so whomever Mark was screwing was really none of my business, and I knew this even if it was my best friend. This revelation however, didn't stop me from ordering shot after shot trying to drown my sorrow in the liquor. My life was not at all what I thought it would be. So yeah, I was getting white girl wasted. Hell, I needed this.

Clearly, so did Marcella because she was tossing them back, too. She told me all about how she and Lance were basically co-existing. She told me that she knew for sure that he was messing around. She even told me that she wasn't sure if it was with men or women and that she really didn't care. Now, I was waving my damn napkin in her face.

"So, Marcella, for-real, you don't care if your husband is messing around on you? And please don't tell me you think that it could be with a damn man. What the fuck, Mar?" I realized how judgmental I sounded and immediately regretted saying it, but it was too late, Marcella's eyes were already tearing up. She reached for her tissue to wipe her eyes and spoke through the tears she was desperately trying to choke back.

"Christian, I really don't... give... a... fuck. I wish Lance would fall in love with whomever he spends his time with and leave. I would help him pack his shit and drive the moving truck through a blizzard with a bathing suit on, barefoot in the middle of the night simply to get rid of his ass. Do you hear me? I would carry every damn box on my back into his new place. I want him gone." She paused and I thought better of saying anything.

We paid the bill and headed for the parking lot. I gave Marcella the tightest hug that my arms would allow me. There was something in Marcella's eyes that worried the hell out of me. I knew that look. I knew what it felt like to be trapped in your own pain. Damn did I know. I didn't know what to do for her. Why was there a black cloud hanging around me and my peeps? I really felt we deserved a break.

I drove home in no big hurry. Hell things at that place weren't so great either. I thought about Marcella, and then my mind turned to Mark, then back to Marcella. I called Kory, and of course he didn't answer. While I was busy asking Marcella if she thought her marriage could be saved, I ought to be asking myself that very same question. I had a husband that wouldn't even answer the phone when I called. It was easy for me to picture Lance being downstairs and Marcella being upstairs all the time because truth be told, that's what Kory and I did.

My heart was starting to beat quickly, and I was beginning to have trouble breathing. I knew this feeling, too; it's a panic attack. I let all the windows down and immediately pulled over. I sat there for a few minutes, trying to think happy thoughts. Anything to restore normalcy. I checked my phone to see if Kory had called back even though I knew damn well it didn't ring. I checked for text messages; nothing. I simply laid my head back and thought about KJ. I always thought about him when I needed to calm down. After about 10 minutes, I felt well enough to at least drive home. I'd tried Kory at least three times along the way. Nothing. His voice mail was full, so I couldn't leave a message, but he saw my number.

Not more than 10 minutes after I got in the house, Kory walked in. The sight of him made me angry, particularly because he walked in on the damn phone. Now, Marcella just got through telling me that Lance talked to his chicks in front of her. Well, it's not going down like that around these parts. While he was still standing in the hallway just as attentive to his conversation as could be, I picked up my phone and called him. It's a damn shame that we were not more than 12 feet away from one another, but I had to call him to get his attention.

CHAPTER 10

Cassandra, the bride-to-be, was pleased that I offered to throw a dinner in honor of her upcoming marriage to my father. She provided me with the names and addresses of a few of her friends living in the Detroit area that she wanted invited, but mostly it would be our family and friends as most of her friends and family resided in Arizona.

I called on my friend Shauna who had recently gone into the event planning business and told her what I was trying to do; she set everything up and to my surprise, Kory paid the bill, no questions asked. I hadn't seen Mark since the day of my client Melissa's wedding, and this dinner would definitely be difficult. Everyone would be there, so

Mark and I had to be extremely careful. No runs to the store, getting chairs from the basement, none of that shit.

Kory and I had actually been getting along well ever since we attended Melissa and Donte's wedding. I actually got out of the shop in time to make it. Kory was cool with Donte, so he was all up for attending. Sitting there listening to Melissa and Donte take their vows did something to me. I remembered the feeling I got when the pastor pronounced them man and wife. Kory took my hand and squeezed it, and I felt the love that the man that I'd married transferred from his hand to mine. It was true that I had some wicked feelings for Mark, but I was married to the man God sent for me.

As I listened to the pastor talk about true love, my love for Kory was reaffirmed. I had loved that man since the day I laid eyes on him. It wasn't the same type of love that I had for Mark, but Dr. Wardelle had helped me understand that. I clung to Mark because I felt like I had no one else. My grandmother hated me, I felt like my father was obligated to love me, and my mother abandoned me. Mark was a constant in my life, and that's what I needed at the time, no matter how wrong it was. I didn't need Kory, I wanted him, and that was the difference. That was the difference that I had to recognize so that I could dismiss this thing with Mark and get back to loving my own husband wholeheartedly.

Not to say that I hadn't thought about Mark from time to time. I knew he could tell that I was pulling away because one day he got drunk and called my cell phone talking shit on my voicemail. I didn't answer because I didn't trust myself, but he blew my voicemail up. It was going to be a hard process because although Mark and I had gone a very long time without sexual contact, we hadn't ever really put an end to our thing. But now, it was time to put an end to it. I had to get back to honoring the vows that I took with Kory Jamar Banks, my own damn husband. Melissa and Donte's wedding had been a turning point in our marriage.

When I got to the loft and walked inside, tears filled my eyes; Shauna had laid this place out. It was so pretty. Every candle was in place, the tables were set to perfection, the band was playing, and everything was perfect. I found Shauna in the kitchen directing the caterers and gave her a hug. Shauna had been a faithful client of mine for a few years, and she knew how much my father meant to me. She understood how important this dinner was. I was wishing my daddy and his bride-to-be good luck, but I was also saying thank you. I needed this dinner to show my daddy how much I loved him and that a thousand Carmens didn't add up to one Melvin. So far, Shauna had exceeded my expectations and was definitely helping me with my unspoken apology to my daddy.

As the guests started to arrive, appetizers were being served, and I was beginning to get nervous; Mark and Jasmine weren't there yet, and I sort of hoped they wouldn't come. But about fifteen minutes before dinner, I saw their son Mekhi and he said his parents were right behind him; Jasmine and Mark were on the way.

I must admit, Jasmine looked nice. I never really paid too much attention to her because I always thought of her as being corny, but she was looking kind of fly this evening. Did this bitch have on red bottoms? It didn't matter much to me if she did because I damn sure had on mine. Now Jasmine wasn't going to outdo me at my father's shit. I remember Mark telling me that Jasmine was obsessed with me and was biting my style. I saw it now. Auntie Jas had stepped up her game. But there'd always be only one

Christian and that was me, so she could dye her hair to match mine, shop wear I shop, ask Mark to call her Christian or whoever but she better recognize: Auntie Jas needed to stay in her own goddamn lane.

Jasmine spoke first. "Hello Christian, what a nice job you've done to honor your father," she said all polite and shit.

I could've smacked the smirk off of her face, but before I could even say, thanks, Mark came over. "Well look what you've done here. You never cease to amaze me. You've done well, baby girl," he said. I think he would have been okay, but the 'baby girl' comment touched a nerve with his wife.

I'd been working out and knew that I looked good in my cocktail dress that hugged the shit out of my curves. Mark was looking. I knew it, and she knew it.

"I would hardly classify her as a baby," Jasmine said, pretending to be joking. I turned around and let them both watch my ass jiggle as I walked away. Damn right, a baby don't have ass like this.

Everyone was there by the time dinner was ready to be served. I quickly made a restroom run. I wasn't surprised when I heard the door open right after I'd gone into the stall. I saw those bottoms and knew it was Jasmine. She didn't go into the stall, so I assume she was waiting for me, but I hoped she was freshening up her makeup. When I came out of the stall to wash my hands, she stared me up and down. Then it started.

"You think you're something, huh? You think that you can do whatever the hell you want to do with no consequences. Don't you? You think that because you stole Mikala's husband and everyone went along with it, that you can have any man you want, don't you?"

I continued to wash my hands and ignore her ass. Then she turned off my damn water. She knew I'd say something to her then.

"Look, Jasmine, I don't know what you're talking about. Yes, Kory was married to Mikala when I started seeing him. It was wrong, but it's really none of your business, now is it?" I turned my water back on to rinse the remaining suds off my hands. I dried my hands and begun to freshen my makeup all the while this crazo was staring at me.

"You think I am stupid?" She was starting to raise her voice now, but I wasn't going to let Jasmine take me there, not tonight anyway.

"No, Jasmine, you're one of the smartest people I know. What I do think is that you're beating around the bush. If you have something to say to me, say it. Say what the fuck is on your mind because as soon as I finish my makeup, I am going back out to celebrate the upcoming wedding of my father. Now, again, what's on your mind, Auntie?" I asked, taunting her ass.

"What kind of woman, are you? Huh? What kind of woman would have sex with her own uncle? You two are some sick individuals, and I bet that daddy of yours wouldn't be so happy to know that you didn't lose your virginity to Alan. I am sure he'd be curious to know who your first really was."

I was shook like a mutha, but I remained so cool and calm. "Mark told me you were sick and had made sick accusations. You're jealous of me, always have been. Too bad, Jasmine. Think what the fuck you want to think. I am going out to sit next to my husband and have dinner. I suggest you do the same." With that I walked out the bathroom. I was shaking, and my heart was skipping beats.

Dinner was delicious and uneventful, but that's because the liquor had yet to be served. Mark looked nervous when he realized that Jasmine and I had been alone together. I shot him a quick look to let him know that things were not good.

My daddy and Cassandra were elated. There were so many congratulatory messages. Everyone was having a good time, and then the bartenders began pouring the liquor. Kory and I had danced so hard that I started to sweat. Of course Mark had too much to drink, probably due to his nerves and kept twirling Jasmine's ass right over there by Kory and me. Finally, I broke the dance and went onto the back patio for air. Kory stayed inside and talked to several of his friends who'd showed up to show Mel love. I was out there alone for a few minutes before Mark started texting me, telling me how nice I looked in my dress. How he wished he had been the one dancing with me instead of

Kory. How he knew it was over, but he wanted to make love to me one last time. All types of shit. This was the shit I wish he wouldn't do. I didn't text back, but that only made him text me more. As I was deleting his last text, Jasmine joined me on the patio. She too had been drinking, but didn't appear drunk.

"What does he see in you? You're a tramp. You've always been a tramp."

"Look, Jasmine, I am not going to take much more of your shit tonight. I think you should find Mark and mind your own damn business."

"Who Mark sleeps with is my business." She was starting to raise her voice.

"Maybe so," I said, "but that's between you and Mark. I ain't got shit to do with your love life."

"Oh no? You have been fucking him since you were what? Thirteen." I kept walking to other parts of the patio, but she kept following me.

"What the fuck are you talking about? You've had too much to drink. I would appreciate it if you would leave now." I was getting nervous because this bitch wasn't letting up.

"Your grandmother told me everything a long time ago. Why do you think she was so gung ho on me and Mark getting married? She wanted him to get away from you. But it didn't work because my husband left me on my fucking wedding day to be with you. What type of man does that? She told me everything. I know about the abortions, Christian.

"She caught y'all in the fucking act more than once. I know about the college visits. Mark was always down there talking about frat business. Frat business my ass. He

222

was down there to see you. I saw him on top of you my damn self in your basement at your graduation party, but when I questioned him about it, do you know what he did? Do you?"

I was speechless. I knew we'd been uncovered, and as cool as I tried to play it off, I knew that Jasmine could read my face. She knew. She'd known all along. I couldn't understand why she waited this long to confront me. I kept my poker face and repeated, "You are one sick bitch, like my damn grandmother. Fuck y'all."

"Do you know what he did to me?" she repeated. "He kicked my ass to the floor. My nose and jaw was broken during that fight. He put his hands on me when I'd said something against his precious Christian. He was livid. He couldn't even really apologize for it. He meant every hurtful word he said and each blow that came with them."

"Good night, Jasmine."

"Oh, tramp, you are going to stand here and listen to what I have to say, you can either listen out here where it's me and you, or you can listen in there in front of everyone," she threatened. She had me by the balls, so I stood there and listened.

"Please look me in the eye and tell me that you are not fucking my husband." I was about to open my mouth, but she quickly jumped in. "Don't lie to me," she yelled.

"What do you want me to say, Jasmine? He's my uncle, and no, I have not had any inappropriate relations with him. Yeah I love him, but so do all my other cousins. For the last damn time, he is my uncle and I am his niece, probably even his favorite niece. But that is it. Now miss me with the rest of this shit. Go take your crazy meds or whatever the hell you need and get the fuck out of my face."

She took another drink as the bartender walked by and gulped it down. She did not heed to my warning; in fact, she had gotten a bit bolder and came all in my personal space. "What is it?" she asked, touching my face. "He likes this face." Then she started running her fingers in my damn hair. "He likes your hair. I have the same hair. She sniffed my neck. "I wear this perfume."

She had completely lost her damn mind. She should not drink ever again. She was getting quieter now, which scared the hell out of me. I didn't even move. Do you know this heffa reached her hand in my dress and grabbed my damn breast and said, "I even paid to get some of these. Why doesn't my husband like me? Why would he rather make love to you than to me?" She was crying now. She repeated herself a million times and still hadn't taken her hand out of my damn dress.

My daddy taught me well, and although I was shaking in my fifteen hundred dollar shoes, I kept a straight face. I did feel sorry for her, but enough was enough. I stepped back and that removed her hand from my breast. I tried my best to sound sincere as I lied to her over and over again about how much Mark loved her dumb ass. "Look, none of the things my grandmother told you about me and Mark are true, Jasmine," I said. I was more than ready to end this conversation. The only person ever to get me to admit anything that happened between me and Mark was Dr. Wardelle, Carmen, and God, and I was sorry that I'd confessed the shit to Carmen; she didn't care no way. I don't give a rat's ass what my grandmother's evil soul told her or what she'd seen. Hell, I didn't care if Mark confessed to his beloved wife; I was going to my grave keeping my lips sealed.

"Jasmine, I am really sorry that my convoluted grandmother made up all those stories and then shared them with you. I knew she hated my mom and me, but I thought she liked you. I can't understand why she would have told you those things knowing they'd hurt you. She thought the world of Mark, so again, I don't know why she'd put him in this mess. Something was clearly wrong with her.

"I think she might have been bi-polar or something like that. But again, none of this is true. Like Mike, Marlon and Mario are my uncles, Mark is my uncle. That's it. He's the baby, and yes, we are close, but he's my uncle. You can take it or leave it, but I am done talking about it. Now I am going to go back out there and party with my daddy.

As I walked away, I heard her through her sobs, "Christian, was Kory Jr. my husband's son? Was he?" I never looked back.

I had spoken boldly, but my confidence was anything but. Jasmine shook me to my damn core. When I reentered the party, I was elated to see that everyone was having a great time. I could tell the liquor had been pouring freely. My father and Cassandra were working the room, and Terri was taking pictures of everything and everyone. I couldn't let this little shit with Jasmine ruin my night. I walked over to Kory who was talking to Lance, which seemed unusual.

"Hey Mrs. Banks," Lance said like we were cool.

"Japs," I replied dryly.

Kory looked at me and shook his head. As I was starting to walk away, I heard that nigga say something about me always having my nose in the air. I whipped my neck around so quickly. "For real, for real, Lance? You got something you'd like to say to me?" I said. "You really want to worry about my nose? Where the fuck do you keep *your* raggedy ass nose?" He was standing there looking stupid now.

"Christian, leave it alone," said Kory, the god damn saint.

"That's what I thought."

Marcella came over to see what was going on. "What's up, Christian?" she said quietly.

"Tell your husband not to say shit else to me. That's what's up." I saw the look of despair on Marcella's face. Lance came and grabbed her by the arm and led her out the patio where Jasmine had just confronted me about my biggest demon.

But Jasmine had now found her way inside and was strutting over to me and Kory. "You think you can say anything you want to anybody, don't you?" she asked.

"What are you talking about, now?" I quietly asked. Adrenaline flooded into my veins as I bit my bottom lip.

"Excuse me, everyone, may I have your attention please." Mark said from the front of the room. "Attention! Attention! May I have all your eyes and ears to the front of the room?" I stopped my conversation with Jasmine and turned toward the front.

"Greetings friends and family, it's wonderful to see so many of you. For those of you who don't know me, I'm Melvin's baby brother Mark. Please raise your glasses and join me in a toast. We are to here tonight to celebrate the upcoming nuptials of Cassandra and Melvin as they embark together on life's great voyage, marriage. Cassandra and Mel, I'm so happy for the two of you. May your life be filled with inner joy, peace, and contentment." Mark walked over to Daddy and Cassandra and gave them each a hug.

I was truly touched by Mark's words.

"Kiss, Kiss, Kiss!" The crowd started chanting as my father leaned over and kissed Cassandra's lips and then he snorted at me with a grin, his eyebrows crooked.

Jasmine leapt from her chair and raced to the front of the room where Mark was standing. I became slightly jealous as she wrapped her arms around Mark and planted a kiss right on his lips. My face reddened. I looked to my glass and tried to hold back my frown. Mark must have caught my look from the corner of his eye because he damn near pushed Jasmine off of him. I shot him daggers with my eyes as I felt Jasmine's lips curl upwards on her mouth as if she enjoyed torturing me. I looked up at Mark with my eyebrows raised; he winked at me and then gave me a sly look. I didn't notice who caught it because I was still tense, glued to my chair, eyes on Mark. He caught my unpleasant gaze and smiled at me, flashing his teeth.

"I'm ready to go," I turned to Kory and said before Jasmine had the opportunity to start some more shit tonight. I walked over and gave Daddy a hug and said goodbye then turned and hugged Cassandra before Kory and I snuck out the door.

CHAPTER 11

I'm tired; it had been a long week of very little sleep between meeting Cassandra's family, running around helping her with last-minute wedding preparations, and my kids staying up all night; my body needed rest. Kory's parents and Marcella flew down to Arizona for the wedding early Friday morning, and as soon as they were checked in and settled into their hotel, they drove to our hotel to pick up the kids, which allowed me and Kory two days of free time.

Overall the wedding turned out beautiful; the love and energy Daddy and Cassandra brought to the room felt like love again for the first time. When the ceremony began, I felt a little nervous for him. I could tell Daddy was nervous, then it came to the part of the ceremony where they exchanged their vows, and I began to cry. I must have swallowed a million times, desperately trying to swallow down the tears. I didn't want to lose it in front of Cassandra's family, Cassandra, or Daddy. I wiped the tears away as quickly as I could and pulled myself together.

After the ceremony, I went to hug Cassandra and Daddy. I was truly happy for them; I could tell that Cassandra really loved my dad. Cassandra looked absolutely stunning. Her dress was beautiful; it looked as it was made for her. The dress was white with a simple pink bow around the waist, and the veil had a silver lining and small pink gems flowing down it. The strings of pearls and casual hairstyle she wore went right along with the biggest smile on her face.

The dimly lit reception hall was filled with balloons that were spread throughout the room. The tables were covered in a silver tablecloth with pink butterfly decorations on each table. The wedding cake sat on a beautifully decorated table; it was made of white icing with delicately designed edible silver butterflies around it. I took all this in as I listened to the beautiful soft melody being played by the pianist in the corner. Daddy was all in tears during our father-daughter dance. He picked a country song called *My Little Girl*. I am not a fan of country music, but the lyrics were so perfect for us. It's a song about a father remembering special moments with his daughter, while trying to let go. Dancing with my father and listening to that song brought back many happy memories of us.

By the time we got home on Sunday, I was running off fumes, I was glad that Mama Lez decided to take the girls home with her from the airport. I peeled my sweater off and walked upstairs toward our room. I changed into a pair of shorts and a t-shirt, tied my hair up, and made my way back downstairs to the kitchen as Kory was walking in the back door with the mail in his hand. He dropped the mail on the counter and on top laid a white envelope with my name written on it. I didn't even need to look at the sender because I recognized Carmen's writing instantly. I stood there for a few moments, frozen in place. For the life of me, I couldn't figure out why Carmen would be mailing me anything. I quickly tore the envelope open and pulled out the half sheet of paper.

Christian,

I'm so sorry I left. I couldn't stay any longer. You must think I'm a coward, and I feel terrible. I promise I'll come back to visit you, but for now, I need to go back to the place I call home. By the time you get this letter, I will be back in California.

Carmen

I didn't immediately process what I'd just read. I stood for a long moment, staring down at the paper as I reread it. After a few more minutes, it finally sunk in. My eyes locked with Kory's as my lips pulled back from my teeth in a snarl.

"That BITCH!" Crumpling the note, I ran up the stairs to my bedroom, grabbed my cell phone, and dialed Carmen's cell phone. But of course, this was all I got: *Sorry*

I couldn't get your call, but leave a name and a number, and I'll be sure to get back to you later!

The next morning while Kory was still in the bed sleep, something he usually did on Monday's especially after we made love, I called Mama Lez because I knew she would be up early, and we talked about the note Carmen sent me and also about how Kory was cussing and bitching about the possibility that Carmen threw away the five thousand dollars he spent to furnish her apartment for her to only live in there for three months. I told her I was going over to Carmen's apartment to see if she had really left. I asked her if the girls could stay another night and that I would come over early in the morning to get them dressed for school; she agreed. Even though I didn't have the best relationship with my mother-in-law, I couldn't deny that she was a great grandmother; she loved all her grandkids. After

237

we hung up, I jumped in the shower, jumped out, got dressed, put on my make-up, fixed my hair, grabbed my jacket, and walked out the door. I didn't sleep much last night; my mind was so consumed with thoughts of Carmen that I'm glad she didn't answer the phone when I called her because I knew my emotions would have gotten the best of me.

I drove as quickly as I could to Carmen's apartment without endangering the cars in front of me. When I arrived at her apartment, I sat in my truck holding my breath, trying to calm down. As I exited my truck and walked toward her building, I took some more calming breaths. *It's fine. Everything is fine*, I silently said to myself.   I stepped on the elevator with a few other people that were engaged in their own discussion about the long lines at the grocery store. I smiled at them, still trying to calm. I stepped off the elevator on the third floor, and as I approached

Carmen's door, I took a deep breath before knocking.

"Aren't you Carmen's daughter?" A lady walking past wearing a white shirt that had ruffles all the way around the collar stopped and asked me.

"Yes."

She blinked at me confusingly. "Oh, you didn't know? She doesn't live there no more. She moved away, so there's no need to keep knocking." Her words swelled deep into my heart, making me feel fuzzy. Swallowing, I found the courage to look up from the hard stare I had on her shoes. "Is something wrong?" she asked, raising her eyebrow high on her forehead.

Slowly my lips curled into a fake smile. "No nothing is wrong. I was supposed to meet my cousin over here," I lied. My voice was harsh even to me.

"Oh okay, a lot of the stuff in there may be gone because she told a few people in the building they could have whatever was left in there. The door is unlocked."

My eyes began to water up, and with an angry grunt, I pushed the apartment door open, making it my purpose to look in the opposite direction of where this lady was standing. When I walked in the apartment, a lump immediately formed in my throat and an ache in my heart. My lower lip began trembling as I stared at the boxes that were stacked on top of each other against the wall. I pulled my phone out of my purse and dialed Carmen's cellphone. The phone rang a couple of times before the voicemail finally picked up.

At the beep, I said, "Carmen, yeah, this is Christian. At this point in my life, I have come to the realization that you don't give a FUCK about me. The level of humiliation

I've experienced including having arguments with my husband and my father for bringing you here has been very challenging. This has been very stressful and painful, but I'm finding a way to put my life together. Bringing you into my life has truly altered my life, but I have Kory and the kids that I live for, and my focus now is on the ones who care about me. Have a good life and save the excuses for someone who cares." I pushed the end button and threw the phone back into my purse.

I reached for my phone again, this time my fingers trembling as I began typing my text message. *Meet me at Carmen's apartment NOW. She's really gone.* I hit send and continued to sit on the on the couch, trying to get my heart to sink back down to where it was supposed to be. I turned on the television and began watching my favorite episode of *The Cosby Show*, the one where Denise copies a designer shirt for Theo to wear on his date. This had to be the funniest episode ever, and my loud laughter showed how much I was enjoying watching it. There was a knock at the door right before my favorite part, when Theo walks in Denise's room wearing the shirt saying, "Look at these sleeves! My arms are the same length, why aren't my sleeves? The collar's all crazy and it's ten sizes too big!" I was laughing so hard tears were forming in my eyes as I stood and walked over to open the door. He walked in hugging me and pecking me on the cheek.

"Who's here?" he asked.

"Us, me and you," I replied as he turned me around, placing his arms around my stomach then he quickly swung me back around and sucked my bottom lip into his mouth. I hadn't expected it and didn't kiss back because I was not big on kissing. My mind was in another place, but I missed moments like this, and his lips were so aggressive that I began kissing him back. He bit my lip and backed me up against the wall. Something about the way he kissed me and how it felt was turning me on. The throbbing between my legs turned into a heavy pulse that made my entire body stiff. I wanted to slow my body down or maybe try to catch my mind up. Whichever came first didn't matter to me; all I knew was at that moment my thoughts and body were not on the same page. All I was focused on was what was going to happen next. Each time his tongue pushed into my mouth, I imagined it pushing inside of me down there, and I wondered if his tongue would feel as warm as it felt right now if it was between my thighs.

"H-hhmmuh." My breath shook as he pressed me hard against the wall. The muscles in my legs tightened; it was getting hard to stand. I tried to say something, but his mouth interrupted me, and his lips swallowed my words. We knocked against the wall, and I was sure the neighbors heard my moans.

"Take your pants off," he commanded.

I was overwhelmed and waaaay too turned on. It was hard to think straight, but the instant he pulled his hands out from the back of my jeans, I did what he said. It took me a second to figure out how to unbutton my pants, but when I remembered, I unzipped them as fast as I could as he helped me wiggle out of them. His fingers began to tickle the fabric of my underwear that was now sticking to the skin between my legs. He slid his hand across my breast. I could feel my heart pounding against his palm. It made my heart beat even harder knowing he could feel it. I didn't want him to stop because it felt so good.

"Oh my God," I whispered as every single one of my stomach muscles tightened. My body was shaking, and I didn't care that I was being loud. He now had me flipped over on all fours, and my legs were spread wide. I screamed out again, even louder as he pounded the shit out of me.

"Mark," I tried to say his name in between a breath but was cut short. The noise I made was a noise I had never made before. It wasn't a scream because it was soft, but it was pretty damn close.

After we finished making love, we lay on the floor, out of breath and gasping for air with our legs intertwined, our bodies pressed perfectly together like puzzle pieces. Tears formed in my eyes for the umpteenth time since last night after reading Carmen's goodbye note.

"This Carmen shit has been a roller coaster ride full of emotions. I've lost weight, gained weight, and my damn hair is shredding." I chuckled.

"Baby girl, it's going to be all right, you made it this far without her, and you will continue to make it. My brother did an excellent job raising you. Carmen has some soul searching that she needs to do. Only she knows what she's going through and what she's running away from. So

245

don't allow her actions to make you be someone or something you're not."

I replied with a deep sigh as I sat straight up. "I've lost all my mental focus worrying about how she and I were going to mend our relationship, and the BITCH up and ran off anyway." We laughed hysterically in unison as we looked at each other. We sat there and didn't say anything for a while. We knew what we did was wrong on all levels, but it felt so right. Mark stood, bending down to pick up his boxers and pants.

"I'm going to get in the shower really quick," he said. I nodded and smiled because I considered joining him but decided against it and would take a shower when he was finished. It was mid-afternoon when I arrived at Carmen's apartment, and when we left, the sun was beginning to set. I had six missed calls from Kory, so I knew I was going to hear his mouth when I got home.

Mark means so much to me. I missed him. It had been close to two months since we last spoke; it was sudden, selfish and completely unexpected of me to ignore his calls after our last time together at Carmen's apartment after she up and moved back to California. I didn't think anyone could imagine the pain I was going through at the time, and having sex with my uncle didn't make the situation any better. I needed time to sort things out, to find a way to truly end this thing Mark and I had rekindled.

As I stood in the bathroom of the home I shared with my husband and kids, I read over the text message I received from Mark, *Christian, when you get this please call me back. I need to talk to you. I love you.* I hadn't responded to any of the text messages that Mark sent me over the last few months, but I knew I needed to reply to him because I wasn't sure what he would do next.

When I walked out the bathroom, Kory was already in bed, snoring away. I walked over to his side of the bed and gave him a kiss on the cheek. "Good night, baby." As I walked to my side of the bed, I replied to Mark's message. I didn't have the courage to talk to him face-to-face, so I replied through text message, *I cannot do this anymore, and I will not be calling you.* When I finished typing and sending the text message to Mark, I turned the ringer off on my phone and placed it gently on the nightstand and cuddled up next to my husband and began to fall asleep.

When I woke up in the morning, Kory was gone, and there was a note left stuck to the headboard: *Early client, see you later at the shop. Love you babe, Kor.*

I picked up my cellphone to check the time; it was a little past seven. Thank God it was Tuesday; that meant my first client didn't come in until 11 a.m. I rolled myself over and began looking at my missed phone calls on my cellphone. Most of them were from clients that I had missed the previous day and a couple were from Mark, no emergencies so I set my phone back down and decided to get fifteen more minutes of sleep before waking up the girls for school, something Carmen used to do on a daily basis. Carmen's leaving hurt us all in ways she didn't understand, and I refused to sugarcoat her behavior. A couple of months had passed with no word from her at all. I knew this sounded awful, but I truly wished something bad happened to her because of her selfish actions. I tried to call her a few times the first week she left, but after several calls with no answer or return call, I stopped calling. I guess this was my karma for the way I was treating Mark and Kory.

I never wanted my kids to experience the pain Carmen had put me through; they asked about her quite often, but why wouldn't they because she was a part of their daily life. I was tired of hearing, "Where is Grandma?" or

"Can we call Grandma?" I didn't like to intentionally lie to my kids, and this situation wasn't going to change me, so my answer to them was, "Grandma left and she's not coming back." Carmen was out of my life once again without any fair warning.

Chapter 12

Itended to be late to pretty much everything I've ever attended except my appointments with Dr. Wardelle; I was always an early bird when it was time for counseling. With fifteen minutes to spare until pouring out my soul to the man who had become like family, I sat in my car in the parking lot, listening to Marsha Ambrosius' CD *Late Nights & Early Mornings*. When "Far Away" began playing, tears formed in my eyes; this song always reminded me of KJ. He would always remain in my heart and soul. I missed my baby so much; he was one of the greatest creations in my life. I loved my daughters as well, and it brought me to tears when I thought about the possibility of having a life without them, but I had finally learned and accepted that I could love my daughters with everything in me without taking anything away from the portion of my heart that belonged solely to Kory Jamar Banks, Jr.

I had to be a better mother and wife. I mean, I wasn't bad at either, but I felt like there was so much more I could do, and I was just not doing it because for so long, I lived in grief over the loss of my son and lately my time and energy had been focused on Carmen and of course, Mark. There isn't a relationship completely protected from affairs and when I thought about my marriage, I reminisced about all of the things Kory and I had gone through infidelity on both our parts, losing our first hair salon, and of course, dealing with the tragic death of our first born and only son, KJ. We both stuck around when other married couples would have said, "I'm getting the hell out of here."

Realistically, we were both ready to give up on the marriage plenty of times as well. I checked out emotionally for a long time after my son was killed. Kory definitely deserved the award for keeping our marriage together. What was I thinking? My love for Kory was real and because I'd known that all along, even when I was ready to bail on him and the kids, I knew I had to stay. With Kory and our girls was where I was supposed to be. We were finally in a place in our lives where things were going smoothly. Okay, smooth was not the right word, but things were better between us. Maybe calm was a better word. Our communication had really gotten better. We had learned to stay quiet until we were calm enough to work our problems out maturely. I sat deep in thought for a few more minutes before getting out of the car and heading to the office where I'd be in a world of trouble if the walls could talk.

I waddled into the office building that had become like my second home. Gosh, how much money had this man made off of my messed up family?

"Hello." I smiled, waving at the security guard who now knew me on a first name basis as I proceeded to the elevator.

I knocked on the door leading to Dr. Wardelle's office. I was nervous. It was after hours, so Rebecca the administrative assistant was gone for the day. A chill settled in the pit of my stomach as I second-guessed myself about keeping this appointment. I didn't know why, but I still got nervous before each visit. I thought about making a full turn and running back out to my car, but in my condition that wasn't an option. It was proven too late to change my mind when I heard the mellow voice coming from the office. "Mrs. Banks, enter."

Dr. Wardelle looked up from the papers he was reading and arched an eyebrow at me. "Mrs. Banks, it's nice to see you." He smiled. "I see congratulations are in order."

"Hello Dr. Wardelle," I replied. I couldn't look at him yet. This was going to be a hard session. There were reasons why I had stayed away from counseling so long. I guess it was time to reveal all that had been going on, but I didn't know where to begin.

He looked back down at the papers in front of him; he quickly scribbled a note and stacked them aside. I could tell he, too, didn't know what to say.

"Have a seat, Christian. Are you comfortable? Can I get you something to drink?"

I felt a lump in my throat; I was feeling sick as hell. This session was a bad idea. I was not ready for it. "Water would be fine, thank you, Doc," I answered, my voice barely audible. I was out of breath, tired, and uncomfortable. I was definitely not in the mood to discuss this latest episode of my life with him at all.

"It's been a while since our last session. I think it's been what, three or four months? So tell me, Christian," he paused and looked me up and down, "what's been going on since the last time we spoke?" He leaned back in his chair as he eyed me shivering in my seat. For the first time in a very long time, I briefly looked around his office; the room was dimly lit with a few still life paintings on the walls. It seemed as if the decorator didn't want anything too stimulating, perhaps as to not upset the patients that would sit there.

We sat in silence for a moment. Dr. Wardelle stared at me; I stared absentmindedly at the floor. "Where do you want to start?" I asked. I really knew where he wanted to start, but I wasn't ready to go there.

"Wherever you want to start," he said. I said nothing.

"Let's begin by catching up on the Carmen situation," he finally said, sensing that cat literally had my tongue.

I was grateful for his suggestion of talking about Carmen because that was an easy conversation. I could do that. "As far as Carmen is concerned, I will never know the truth behind her leaving me thirty something years ago because my daddy told me she left after her stay in rehab, but when I mentioned that to her, she looked at me like she didn't know what I was talking about and gave me a different story." I let out a defeated sigh as Dr. Wardelle's eyes bored a hole into my head. I wanted to look away, but I couldn't.

"Have you ever thought maybe your father told you his version of why Carmen left to save you from additional hurt and emotional pain?" I stared at him, thinking hard about the words he said. A flash of realization overtook my face; I wanted to know what was going through Dr. Wardelle's mind. I wanted him to tell me exactly what I needed to do to get past this Carmen situation and be done with her. Anything else besides asking a million questions about how I felt about every damn thing. There was a long silence as Dr. Wardelle and I were both lost in our own thoughts. "What's on your mind?" he asked, finally breaking the silence.

"I... um... I don't know who to believe. What kind of mother abandons her child? All I know is Carmen left for whatever reason. She said my daddy was cheating and was never there to help her out, and he said she was addicted to antidepressants and left."

"You've told me yourself that your father was a womanizer, so maybe some of what your mother has said is true." I nodded, knowing quite well what Dr. Wardelle was saying to me was the truth; Daddy was indeed a womanizer. I listened, a sick feeling began growing in the pit of my stomach as Dr. Wardelle rattled off the details of my life to me. I guess I was woman enough to understand why she'd leave Mel, but I was too much of a woman to understand why she left me.

I opened my mouth to say something, but he cut me off. "And then maybe some of what your father said is the truth because you did tell me that your mother admitted to being on drugs. I think both your mother and father have their own versions of what happened." I took a few deeps breaths making an attempt to get myself under control so I wouldn't cry a river in this man's office.

"That's it. There is a secret that I still need to uncover," I blurted out. I wasn't as ready as I thought to discuss the last few months of my life, so I danced around the subject matter at hand.

"What is this about, Christian? Am I missing something obvious because what you're mentioning are conversations we've already discussed?" Dr. Wardelle asked, looking at me with a stale face.

Taking a deep breath, I folded my hands and began speaking. "Okay, how can I explain this? When I came back from my daddy's wedding in Arizona, I received a letter in the mail from Carmen saying that she'd moved back to California. I was so hurt because this all came without warning. The next day I drove over to her apartment to make sure she did indeed leave. I asked Mark to meet me there, and we talked for a while but ended up having sex.

"And from that date until now, I've been avoiding talking to him. I texted him to basically say don't ever call me again. He is not leaving me alone though. He contacts me daily. My uncle is basically stalking me. It's killing me because I want to talk to him. I want to be with him every free moment I have. I have never felt the sense of peace with anyone that I feel when I am with him. He was the first person to love me who didn't have to."

Dr. Wardelle just sat and listened. He'd heard all of this before, so it was no surprise to him I'm sure. I hoped he hadn't become frustrated with me. He was very tactful in the way that he expressed himself, but he was really ready for me and Mark to be over. The problem was I was not. I didn't know that I'd ever be. I began to cry. My cries quickly turned to sobs. I got sick to my stomach just hearing myself say this shit aloud. Tears were streaming down my face, and I couldn't stop crying.

"I know it's sick. I know how much damage we've done and the insurmountable amount of damage we will do if anyone else finds out about us. We are playing a dangerous game with so many lives. Sometimes I want to kill myself to take myself out of this misery. It's a never ending cycle because when I feel like that, it's him and only him that I can turn to.

"Who the fuck else am I going to admit to being depressed because me and my uncle just left a hotel on the outskirts of town having some of the most passionate sex and now he's on his way home to his wife, and I'll be facing my husband soon? You don't just call up your girlfriend and say no shit like that, especially not when your number one girlfriend is your husband's baby sister. So I have to turn to him, right?"

Again Dr. Wardelle and I sat staring at each other in complete, awkward silence.

"Dr. Wardelle, I'm tired of these tears. I'm tired of feeling this way, I'm tired of feeling unwanted by Carmen, and I'm tired of loving Mark in the way we both know that I shouldn't be loving him."

I left out the exchange of words with Jasmine at my father's dinner and also how I was enraged by the way she came at me all confident and shit that night. Then Auntie Jas taunted my ass by hanging all over Mark and there wasn't a damn thing I could do. My only consolation was that he did not reciprocate, and it was obvious. Jas knew that she could get away with that bullshit that night, but let there be no misunderstanding, Auntie knew it was me, Christian that had her husband's attention and more importantly, his heart. She was right; she could blow up the spot and tell the entire family what she thought she knew. But she wouldn't; she couldn't. Her life would be ruined by that announcement as well. Jasmine couldn't handle that type of shame. She simply ain't cut from that cloth. So like me, she was going to play her position despite her suspicions. I guess we all fucked up.

Thinking back to the evening of my father's dinner party, I realized then that I'd end up back in the bed with Mark; Jasmine took me there. It had always been a competition between us for Mark's affection, and I had always won; I'd never been threatened by Jasmine's presence in my uncle's life. He had to play the part, take on a wife, have a couple of kids, get the good job, beautiful home, all that. My grandparents groomed him for that style of living from day one. Jasmine was just part of the façade to me. At my daddy's dinner though, she was on her A-game, and I didn't like that shit one bit. She let me know she wasn't going down without a fight, and she had me by the balls; I couldn't kick my aunt's ass over my uncle's affection. Oh, but I wanted to. I wanted to mop that bathroom floor with that ass. How would we have explained that shit to our guests who included my husband and the guest of honor, my daddy?

Plus, as much as I hated to admit it, she was right. I did think I could have whatever or whomever I wanted and for years I got it. But I couldn't have Mark. No matter how deep my feelings were for him as a man, the reality was that man was my father's baby brother. My mind was screaming at me telling me that I lost. Jasmine's corny ass beat me. I couldn't have Mark Johnson, point...blank...period. I didn't want to talk about this issue any longer, so I quickly tried to change the subject. "Kory and I are doing really good right now," I mumbled randomly.

Dr. Wardelle smiled at me as he folded his hands behind his head. "Christian, you will be in a much better position if you close that chapter of your life that includes Carmen. Maybe you can revisit that relationship in the future, but you need to allow Carmen to reach out to you, and you need to heal from everything that has happened recently. Keep in mind she may never come back around. So you have to find a way to be okay with that."

His words sort of caught me off guard. I was in deep thought about Mark; I damn near forgot we ever discussed Carmen. It took me a second or two to process what Dr. Wardelle said about my mother. I completely understood his concern, and I respected his opinion. I guess I was still trying to pretend that things with Carmen would one day work themselves out because I simply could not think of any other thing to try in order to build a relationship with her. I didn't know what she wanted from me or what I wanted from her. Sometimes I second guessed myself and wondered if I really wanted a mom or was I just drawn to the challenge of trying to make her love me. The more I thought about Carmen over the last few months, the more I realized that my husband and father were right to tell me to leave it alone.

Carmen carried me in her womb, she gave me life, and it stopped there. Carmen was not my mother. Christian Alicia Johnson Banks did not have a mother, and I was okay with that. This was the last visit with Dr. Wardelle that any amount of time would be dedicated to Carmen. I was good. Like my Aunt Whit tried to tell me, Carmen done died on them streets in California; shit, she might as well be dead.

Dr. Wardelle always remained calm, eerily calm and he never raised his voice. He wrote a few notes on his notepad, cleared his throat, and suddenly looked up at me, placing his pen down on the top of the notepad. When he finally spoke, his voice had raised a few octaves, "You and Mark should not be around one another or have any contact with each other." He paused; he seemed to be concentrating for a few moments while he stared at me intently. His gaze was dark and intense, but it was different than the kind he usually wore when upset or disappointed. "Christian, it's

267

time to re-evaluate your own self-worth, self-value, and self-esteem. You have to repair you! And, it starts from the inside out. Hopefully you can learn to forgive yourself so you can forgive those who you feel have hurt you. The relationship with Mark happened, it's done, and now it's over, right?" he asked sternly while shaking his head at me.

"Yes, it's over," I replied, giving him a small, weak smile. I never took my eyes off him. Not for a second. I stared up at him, breathing heavily. I'd just said it was over between me and Mark. Dr. Wardelle might believe me, but I didn't know if I believed myself. He's right about me not valuing myself, I never have. I released that power to my uncle while still in training bras. He'd always been the one to make me feel worthy, special... all that. Ending this thing with Mark frightened the hell out of me. I knew Kory loved me; damn I kept saying that to make myself believe Kory's love was enough, but Mark had my heart long before Kory entered my life. I hoped an obsession would grow for Kory to replace the already developed obsession I had for Mark but it never has. I'd always longed to be loved by Mark. I always believed that as long as our souls were connected to each other, that the flame of our love would burn forever. I swear I used to wish Mel wasn't my father as my grandmother's wicked ass used to always claim. Then Mark and I could have been together.

What was I thinking? Mel would have still raised me and that wouldn't have worked, but damn it would have been better than having an incestuous relationship for the majority of my life. How can I have self-worth when I had gone out of my way to take another woman's husband, only to marry him and never be able to completely give myself to him because a part of me lives in the heart of my own god-damn uncle? *So naw, Dr. Wardelle, I ain't got no self-worth, I don't value myself, hell I ain't really worth nothing. I put on a good front, but let's keep it real; my own mother didn't want me. My father felt obligated to raise me, my grandmother hated my fucking guts, my uncle molested me, and years before we were married, Kory did something unexpected...he beat me up, raped me, left me for dead on our shops floor and after all that I still married him. Where the hell am I supposed to find some self-worth?*

I was in my own world. When Dr. Wardelle spoke, he startled me. My head was heavy. I felt like shit. I should have definitely turned around today. All this damn counseling and I was no better. "It's time to heal, Christian. It's going to take time, it's not going to be easy, and there will be road bumps along the way, but I will be there with you every step of the way." I looked up at Dr. Wardelle and smiled at his comment. "What are you thinking?"

He really didn't want to know what I was thinking. This was who I was. I was a good actress though, and I would always put on a brave face. I would appear as if I had it all together. I would continue to be that bitch Christian in public. I would continue to use my counseling sessions as the one time a month when I could just be myself. When I could admit to myself all of the god awful things I'd done in my life. When I could admit that I had had more sex with my uncle than I had with anyone, including Kory. I had other secrets, too, some that Dr. Wardelle didn't even know about. I guess I'd take those to the grave.

I pulled my car keys out of my purse as I replied, "Dr. Wardelle, I am just thinking that my life has always been a mess, but I am just now beginning to realize that I'm broken, Doc." I wondered again why I just didn't cancel this appointment. That would have been much easier.

Dr. Wardelle saw the defeat in my eyes, he heard it in my voice, and one thing this man did not do was push. I knew he wanted to go back into the self-worth and value speech he prepared just for me, but he didn't. Dr. Wardelle knew in his heart that I was broken, too. We just had to find a way for me to cope with this realization, a way for me to function as a wife, mother, stylist, and business owner. Yep, that's it, a way for me to keep frontin'. I had given up on fixing myself. I couldn't. I didn't know how.

When you shatter a glass into a million pieces, it's virtually pointless to try to reassemble it. I was that broken glass, and even someone as skilled and talented as Dr. Wardelle lacked the competencies to put me back together. We looked at one another for the next few minutes not saying a word, but I knew he was agreeing with me. He looked at me, the way you look at all that damn broken glass on your kitchen floor.

Dr. Wardelle finally spoke, "I know it's the end of today's session, but since you didn't mention it, I would like to ask. Christian, is that Mark's baby you're carrying?"

EPILOGUE

I was in the last month of my pregnancy, and I felt like the days were dragging on. I became tired rather easily. I was also suffering from backaches, and my ankles were swollen beyond recognition. My stomach was huge, and I could not wait until I was back down to my pre-pregnancy weight and able to fit into my regular clothes. Working was nearly impossible. Thank God for my assistants who took over my clients.

Lately my mind continuously thought about who the baby would look like. I had become obsessed with it. When I first learned that I was pregnant again, I almost died. I sank into a deep depression. I cried daily and told no one, not even Marcella. I made several appointments at different abortion clinics in Ohio. I dared not risk going to one here.

But, I couldn't go through with it. The memories of my grandmother forcing me to abort baby after baby when I was a teenager had traumatized me. So as I continued to make and cancel appointment after appointment, I grew further along in my pregnancy. Now, here I was in the hospital where I had given birth to all of my children, getting ready to add one more to the Banks Bunch. I let out a soft sigh as I lay in the hospital bed looking down at my stomach.

"It is amazing," Kory said as he felt the baby kick his hand yet again. This baby was definitely more active than any of my babies. He or she kicked something crazy, and although Kory found it amazing, I found it annoying. This shit hurt. Then the contractions became stronger, and I gave up on the natural birth shit and begged for an epidural. After eleven hours of labor, it was finally time to welcome our fifth child into this world.

Kory had taken his position right next to the doctor at the bottom of the bed, ready to put his eyes on our newest pride and joy. "Chris, the baby is coming now!" he shouted. My panic level rose when I felt yet another sharp pain in my stomach.

"Just one more push and you're done, baby," Kory said as he kept his attention on the baby.

Kelis Simone Banks was born June 16 at 9:35 p.m., seven pounds, two ounces and nineteen inches long. Once she was out and Kory cut the cord, I collapsed against the pillows and closed my eyes.

I was very tired and wanted to fall asleep right then and there, but I was not going to do so until I saw my baby. I was feeling dizzy, but I wanted to see Kelis. He held her up to my face. She was swaddled in that ugly hospital blanket that I hated, and all I could see was her fat brown face. She appeared small as she wiggled around in Kory's arms, crying rather loudly, probably trying to get free from that ugly ass blanket. Then she opened one of her lazy little eyes. Her eye color shocked me. All of my kids had dark brown eyes, so dark that sometimes they looked black. That was something we all got from Carmen, so looking at the hazel color of Kelis' eyes almost sent me into a panic.

I tried to relax by telling myself that kids' eye color could change as they get older. But who was I kidding? Something in my gut told me that Kelis was my hazel-eyed beauty. I just stared at her for a while. All the rest of the family came rushing in and I started to hear pictures being taken while they oohed and ahhed over her. Within minutes, I heard nothing further and drifted off to sleep until I heard Kory's voice.

"Chris!" His voice sounded far away, like he was underwater. I peeked out of one eye and saw his lips moving, but I couldn't tell what he was saying. I saw the lips moving again, and this time I could hear his voice a bit more clearly. "Chris, they are getting ready to move you to the post delivery room. They want to bring Kelis in so that you can feed her," he said. I heard him, but was too out of it to respond. "Are you all right?"

I nodded, and they began to wheel me, bed and all, down the hall to a new room. The nurse met me at the door with Kelis, and for the first time, I was able to take a good long look at the most beautiful thing I'd ever seen, Little Miss Kelis. I was totally in love with her.

I'd seen and experienced a lot of things in my life that could make a regular person's head spin. However, what I was seeing right now was something completely unexplainable. I hated to admit it, but Kelis did not look much like any of my other children. They were all spitting images of one another. Kelis was the spitting image of Mark; they had the same brown complexion, light eyes, and the thickest jet black hair. Now, Karen, my sister-in-law had deep brown skin, too, and of course, the hazel eye gene ran in my family, so it was acceptable for one of my kids to have them as well. I had done the math so many times over the last few months, and although it was a long shot, it was not impossible that the wicked attraction that Mark and I had possibly resulted in another maybe baby, which was why in the beginning I wanted to abort this baby. I just wasn't sure. Kory snapped me out of my daydream.

"She looks like me and KJ, but I see your side of the family in her, too. Doesn't she look like Mel a little bit? And look at her eyes. They are exactly like Mark's and Mekhi's," Kory said. I chuckled to myself. If he thought Kelis looked like him and KJ, I wasn't going to say shit.

I embellished it and agreed. "She looks just like you and KJ," I lied.

I tightened the grip I now had on Kory's hand, the hand that was always willing to save me from anything. Taking a deep breath to settle my overwhelming emotions, I glanced up and smiled at him as I thought of the many nights I stayed up laying in our bed, thinking about how I could get our marriage right. To show Kory just how much I loved him, to tell him just how much he meant to me and to put in words all the love I had for him. Kory reached over and began wiping away my tears.

"You are so beautiful when you cry, but you are even more gorgeous when you smile," he said, leaning in to kiss my forehead.

"I'm going to take the baby back to the nursery to have her vitals read, and I'll be right back, okay?" were the last words I heard the female nurse say before I dozed back off to sleep, still thankful that Kory somehow saw a resemblance between himself and our new princess.

The next morning, my eyes popped opened slightly, and I gasped loudly and barely caught myself from falling off the little ass bed. I couldn't get used to this twin bed, and I guess I had tossed and turned myself damn near off it. In addition, my breasts were sore. Shit, I forgot about this part. I opened my eyes completely and let out a long yawn. I looked warily around the room; the sun streamed through my open window. I was beginning to realize I was still in the hospital. I was still a bit disoriented after last night's dream.

In my dream, Mark and Jasmine tried to take my baby away from me. It was crazy because although it was Jasmine, she looked like Carmen. We were basically playing tug a war with Kelis. I did my best to sit up and look out the window. Kory was standing next to my bed holding a tray of breakfast. *Great, hospital food*, I thought sarcastically. I picked up the card that was next to the bouquet of flowers that were delivered yesterday. I saw all of the beautiful flowers, but I was too tired to read any of the cards last night. The first one I grabbed read *Congratulations on the arrival of your baby girl! We're glad to hear that you and our new grandbaby are doing well.* The card was from Daddy and Cassandra. I talked to him about a week ago, and he told me that he and Cassandra would be in Detroit for the Fourth of July. I couldn't wait for him to meet Kelis.

Well, actually, I wanted Cassandra to meet her, too. It's funny because Cassandra was really irrelevant to me for so long. I hadn't disliked her; I just didn't want to lose her to my daddy. But since their marriage and spending time with her in Arizona, I really got to know her. I actually liked her. She was good for my daddy, and Mrs. Cassandra Johnson had a past. Who would have thought it? She shared things with me that almost made me give her Dr. Wardelle's business card. Now she hadn't sexed her uncle silly, but she wasn't the goody two shoes that I made her out to be. Of course I didn't tell her about half of the shit I'd done in my life, but I was comfortable sharing some things with her particularly the feelings I had about Carmen.

Cassandra shared with me that she had become pregnant in her freshman year of high school, and her mother raised the baby. The young man who I met at their wedding, Uncle Carl, was really my step-brother. Carl was Cassandra's son, not her younger brother. When she told me that shit, I just stared at her in amazement. I couldn't believe my ears. She must have read my mind because she took my hand and told me that she'd told my daddy all about Carl. She told me that Mel basically told her that we all have our shit to bear and that he wasn't no saint, so he wasn't going to judge her about the shit she'd done in the past. My daddy was right; he definitely had a past and he damn sure wasn't no saint.

Cassandra went on to tell me that rebelling, she purposely got pregnant again in her junior year of high school. Damn near knocked my socks off when she told me the father of that baby was some Jewish boy. She cracked me up talking about how fucked up his parents were that their little Gregory had gotten a black girl pregnant. They basically paid Cassandra and her family to put the baby up for adoption. These experiences allowed Cassandra to speak candidly about a subject that I thought I'd never understand; how a mother could give up her child. In this case, Cassandra had given up two.

She helped me understand a lot about what Carmen might have gone through giving me up. She also helped me to see how Carmen's relationship with Kameko had nothing to do with her relationship with me. Even though I often didn't get it, Cassandra told me that it was perfectly reasonable for a mother to love and dote on one child without even knowing another child. I felt like shit. For the first time in my life, I actually felt worse at that moment than I did when I lost KJ. Mark was super supportive, and we both realized that this was it. Our thing had gotten way out of control, and it was time to release it. Mark was fucked up about the possibility of having a child that he wouldn't raise, but understood why he couldn't. We both understood. No matter what, we agreed that this baby was Kory's. Mark swore on his life that he would never try to come between that and would just admire the baby from afar. We'd lived a lie our entire lives, and this would be no different. We continued to talk during dinner, and there was something in me that really felt like it was over between us. I didn't know what it was, but I felt it. It hurt, too. I was sad, but knew it was for the best. When dinner was over, he walked me to my car, no hug, no kiss, just a goodbye.

The knock on my hospital room door snapped me out of my trance and ended Kory's photo shoot with Kelis. In walked the attendant with the most beautiful bouquet that I'd ever seen.

Kory said, "Chris, I think Mel sent you more flowers." He only quickly glanced at the card. He was too busy trying to return to his picture taking. My daddy had just had flowers delivered yesterday. It wasn't like him to send another elaborate bouquet again. I opened the card and read it to myself: *Congratulations Baby Girl on the arrival of what I hear is the cutest little girl in the family. I can't wait to meet her. Love you and Kelis. See you soon, Daddy.* Good thing Kory didn't notice that the floral shop's address was not located in Arizona where Mel lived. Nope, these flowers came from a shop right here in Detroit; I recognized the name all too well. I tucked the card away in my drawer and looked over at Kelis and her daddy.